Chain Links

We're Better Together

Book Set to Songs

John W. Nassivera

Illustrated by John W. Nassivera

ISBN- 978-0-9971079-2-0

Library of Congress Control Number: 2018913349

Printed in the USA

Dedication

In memory of my mother
Susanne E. Cutler Nassivera

Earthbound Angel

Occasionally, we are graced with the presence of an earthbound angel.

They are unable to stay with us for long, but while they do, they bring unprecedented joy and happiness to all they touch.

While they are here, we bask in their goodness and marvel at their contribution to the world.

When they leave, we are left with the devastation that comes with losing such a wonderful being, but we must remember that the earthbound angels are not ours to keep.

They are ours to enjoy, learn from, and behold until they return home.

We love you mom.

Acknowledgements

Thank you to the 2016-17 fourth graders of Mr. Ethan Doak and Mrs. Melanie Healy at the Hudson Falls, NY Intermediate School, who collectively created many of the chapter titles for "Chain Links."

Contents

Chapter 1   One Person's Trash is Another Person's Treasure
Chapter 2   Close Call
Chapter 3   Snap! Clack! Pop!
Chapter 4   Blue Goo
Chapter 5   The Fix
Chapter 6   A Race Against Time
Chapter 7   Rules Are Rules
Chapter 8   An Idea
Chapter 9   It's Show Time
Chapter 10 The Challenge
Chapter 11 Get Out of the Way
Chapter 12 Something to Smile About
Chapter 13 Chance of Rainbow Showers
Chapter 14 Please Give a Warm Welcome
Chapter 15 Drum Roll, Please
Chapter 16 The Winner is…
Chapter 17 Fist of Fifty
Chapter 18 If Not You, Then Who?
Chapter 19 It's Our Secret
Chapter 20 A Cloud of Fury
Chapter 21 All Wet
Chapter 22 Checkmate
Chapter 23 What's This All About?
Chapter 24 A Tightly Knit Circle
Chapter 25 Show the Love

Book Set to Songs

1. **As We Get Bolder** by John W. Nassivera & Bob Bates
2. **Click Snap Pop** by John W. Nassivera & Bob Bates
3. **Don't Stop** by John W. Nassivera & Bob Bates
4. **Rules Are Rules** by John W. Nassivera & Bob Bates
5. **Stick to the Plan** by John W. Nassivera & Bob Bates
6. **Its Show Time** by John W. Nassivera & Bob Bates
7. **Ready Set Go** by John W. Nassivera & Bob Bates
8. **Stopped Red Handed** by John W. Nassivera & Bob Bates
9. **Chance of Rainbow Showers** by John W. Nassivera, Albert Bouchard, David Hirschberg
10. **Feeling So Cool** by John W. Nassivera & Alan Dunham
11. **Drum Roll Please** by John W. Nassivera, Albert Bouchard, David Hirschberg
12. **The Winner Is** by John W. Nassivera & Alan Dunham
13. **Head in A Haze** by John W. Nassivera & Alan Dunham
14. **The Scent of Violets** by John W. Nassivera, Albert Bouchard, David Hirschberg
15. **Grant Me Friends** by John W. Nassivera & Bob Bates
16. **Checkmate** by John W. Nassivera & Alan Dunham
17. **What's This All About** by John W. Nassivera & Bob Bates
18. **Is That a Smile I See** by John W. Nassivera & Bob Bates
19. **Show the Love** by John W. Nassivera & Alan Dunham

Visit www.frontporchstorytelling.com for more information about the songs and artists.

Introduction

Sandy Hill Day was held every September to celebrate the founding of the village. It was a call for community spirit, a day when the entire town came together. Each new year introduced a contest that enabled town residents to showcase the past, present, and future, and today's contest was titled, "Bicycles." First prize was $50, and in 1964, you could do a lot with that kind of money.

Eleven-year-old Tom has been dreaming of taking first place in the bike contest for months. Winning the grand prize would be the answer to his problem. With the help of his friends and several unexpected allies, Tom's bike is ready to go. But, when Tom's friends make a split-second decision that could nullify their qualifications for entering the contest, his dream begins to grow into a nightmare. His mother's voice pops into his head, *It's not what you have that makes you rich, but what you do that lifts you up.* Maybe winning the contest isn't the answer to his problem.

Chain Links

"As We Get Bolder"
John W. Nassivera & Bob Bates

The flyer read, a Bike Contest
The fifty-dollar prize would surely impress
Tom's smile showing his brown eyes squint
Focused on his winning blueprint

Forks scattered out on the concrete
A heap of old parts laid at his feet
Fenders, frames, a dirty old chain
Sick and tired of feeling ashamed

Beauty is in the eyes of beholders
It never fades as we get older
Beauty is in the eyes of beholders
It shines right through as we get bolder

The hands on the clock kept its tick
Tom's little nose smooshed his upper lip
A bit of a shiver went down his spine
Thinking out loud I need more time

I've dream so long of my special goal
The front tire shakes out of control
A J-38 is all I want
Heads will turn as soon as I'm spotted

Beauty is in the eyes of beholders
It never fades as we get older
Beauty is in the eyes of beholders
It shines right through as we get bolder

My bike is nothing more than old worn parts
But we're the ones that work from our hearts
It's not what you have that makes you rich
But what you do when you sew and stich

John W. Nassivera

One man's trash is another man's treasure
There's more here that can be measured
Our friendship with stand cold and ice
Lightning strikes this great place thrice

Beauty is in the eyes of beholders
It never fades as we get older
Beauty is in the eyes of beholders
It shines right through as we get bolder
It shines right through as we get bolder

Chapter 1

One Person's Trash is Another Person's Treasure

The flyer headline read "Sandy Hill Day Parade & Bike Contest," and the $50 first prize would be exactly enough money. Tom's long fingers flipped the leaflet over and pushed his thick, black glasses tightly against his brow. His eyes narrowed, sharply focusing on every detail of the pencil-sketched blueprint for his homemade wheelie bike.

It was 1964, and like every year, the contest brought the entire town together to honor the past, celebrate the present, and look forward to the future. Tom had dreamt about winning the bike contest for months, and in a few hours, the competition would start.

"Where are those two?" Tom asked, looking out the garage door.

The morning's sunlight sparkled off a lime-green bike overturned on the garage floor. The extended front forks stretched out over the concrete, missing a tire. Tom and his friends had spent countless summer days scavenging for the right bicycle parts through trash left for pickup on the local streets. A tire had to be in this twisted, tangled heap of old, salvaged parts.

He couldn't help but remember how much flack he'd taken from some of the kids at school about digging through the trash since they all had new bikes. It got to the point where he was just about to punch Bobby, when he remembered what his mother had said, *It's not what you have that makes you rich, but what you do that lifts you up.*

Tom knelt on one knee and frantically sorted the old parts into fenders, headlights, pedals, frames, and chains. The second hand of a wall clock rhythmically ticked over the sound of his breathing. An anxious, "Grrr….Wrrrao…Maaorrao!" then gurgled and rumbled from his stomach as he came up empty-handed.

"Come in and eat your breakfast!" Tom's mom yelled out the back door. "Your oatmeal is getting cold."

"Oatmeal again," Tom said. "I'm good."

"Good morning, Mrs. Nass," Mike, Tom's sixth grade friend, said as he rolled up to the garage door. "Bummer. You still haven't found a wheelie tire?"

Mike straddled the banana seat perched on a red frame. His blonde crew cut laid tightly above his ears, standing stiff and a half-inch from the top of

4

his head like the bristles of a straw broom. His biceps, which were the size of baseballs, bulged as he tightly squeezed the handgrips.

Frank, another one of Tom's classmates, rolled up and parked beside Mike. His arms loosely hung from the handlebars above his head to his shoulder, making him look like an ape.

"Good morning, Mrs. Nass," Frank said.

"Did you boys eat breakfast?" Tom's mother asked.

The two boys looked to Tom with curiosity as to what his mother had to offer.

Tom's nose smooshed downward into his upper lip. "It's oatmeal again."

"We're good," Mike said. "Thank you."

"That bike is going nowhere," Frank said. "You can kiss the contest goodbye, unless we find the perfect wheelie tire."

"What took you so long?" Tom asked, locking a crescent wrench onto the axle nut and twisting counterclockwise. "I'm running out of time."

Mike raked his fingers through the streamers dangling from the handlebars. "I spotted these cool hand grips on an old bike frame that someone had tossed into the canal. I just had to have them."

"Getting that frame out of the canal was a hassle," Frank said as he dismounted his navy-blue bike and flicked down the kickstand. His husky-sized blue jeans were wet from the ankles to an inch above the knees. A pair of canvas sneakers squished and sloshed with each step, leaving a muddy trail in the garage. His lower lip quivered as a shiver trembled down his spine, and his voice wavered as he said, "That water's freezing."

Tom jumped up and said, "I need help finding the right size tire if I'm going to finish in time." He stomped around to the front of his bike.

"The contest doesn't start until this afternoon," Frank said as he waddled up to the bench. He slipped off one of his water-logged sneakers and nimbly rubbed five wrinkled toes.

"Don't get crazy. We have until 3:00 to register," Mike said.

Tom scratched his head with the crescent wrench, saying, "I just need to stay cool." The rubber heels of his sneakers squeaked across the concrete floor. He stopped at the workbench, stroked the long strands of brown hair off his glasses, and studied the sketch.

"Where do we find a front tire?" Tom said, holding his chin. "We don't have time to search the streets again."

The clinking of metal rang over the rasping of a clunky junk drawer opening from under the bench. Frank foraged his hefty fingers through nuts, bolts, and screws. A wrinkled candy bar wrapper laid half-buried beneath the hardware.

"Ah-ha. Buried treasure," Frank whispered to himself as he tugged the chocolate delight free. He stuffed the booty deep into his front pocket without being noticed.

The ceiling light shimmered off a metal wafer buried in the mishmash of hardware. Frank plucked the silver washer from the bottom of the drawer and held it up in the late morning light.

"This might work," Frank said before tossing it through the air.

Tom caught the washer with one hand. "What are you talking about?" he asked.

6

Frank dug back into the pile and continued to shuffle through the hodgepodge. "Show him, Mike," he said.

Mike dismounted his bike and waved at the chrome sissy bar that rose two feet above the bicycle seat. "What do you think?"

Tom glanced up from the silver washer. "Where did you get that?" He threw the sketch to the benchtop, tucked the washer deep into his front pocket, and raced to the back of Mike's bike. "It's perfect!"

"I thought you'd think so. It's ten inches," Mike said as he fumbled with a knot in the twine that secured the tire to the sissy bar. The twine unraveled, swerving through the rim and swirling over the sissy bar.

Tom squeezed the knobby rutted rubber against his palms, and his fingertips clenched the cold aluminum rim. He ran past the workbench and pulled a ratchet wrench from his father's toolbox. Tom spun the wrench in circles, quickly twisting each nut to the center of the axle. A slight gap between the forks caused the tire to wiggle and wobble as it rotated.

"That tire will jiggle-joggle the bike out of control. You can't enter that in the contest," Mike said.

Frank's head was buried in the drawer, secretly gnawing down the chocolate bar. "Use the washer to close the gap," he mumbled.

Tom twirled the nut from the end of the threaded axle, slid the washer snug against the fork, and spun the nut tight to the last thread. "It worked. I just need one more washer."

Frank smacked his lips. "It has to be here," he said. His fingers shuffled through the mess.

"Let me help." Tom pulled the drawer from the bench and dumped the contents out onto the benchtop. The three friends frantically raked through the clutter and spotted two washers.

Mike held the two side-by-side and said, "The center holes are different."

Tom attempted to slide one of the washers over the axle, but the inside diameter was too small. "I have one last chance," Tom said. The three friends glared urgently at each other. "This has got to work." Tom held the washer to the end of the tire axle. "Here goes nothing."

The washer slid down the axle to the fork. Tom quickly ratcheted the nut to the last thread, tugged with all his might, and compressed the fork snug to the tire. His right hand clamped around the tire and flung it into a spin.

"No jiggle. No teeter. No sway. No wobble." A smile radiated across Tom's face. "Straight as an arrow." Taking one step back and standing tall with his hands resting on his hips, he asked, "So, where did you get this tire?" He looked to the boys and said, "It's perfect for my bike."

Mike chuckled and said, "The same place I got my new handgrips."

"The bike in the canal?" Tom asked.

Frank leaned back against the workbench. "Do you think I'd walk into that cold, muddy water just for a pair of handgrips?"

Tom flipped the wrench into the air. It arced an inch over Mike's crew-cut head, dropped to the bench top, and wobbled to a rest on the blueprint.

Frank pulled the piece of paper from under the wrench, held it at arm's length, and read from a list below the sketch, "Number one, attach front tire." He drew a line through it with a pencil that he'd found in the drawer. "That's done."

Tom smiled. "I don't know how to thank you guys."

Mike waved Tom off, saying, "That's what friends are for."

Frank continued to read, "The last thing left on the list is to tighten the chain."

Mike cranked the pedal, rotating the rickety chain, which clattered, clinked, and clunked over the gears. The faster Mike spun the pedal, the louder the chain rattled.

Frank shifted upward on the stick shifter. The chain's links shuddered across the gear teeth, jerkily trembling the bike frame until the chain snagged and yanked the rear tire to a stop.

Tom pinched the chain between his thumb and index finger and tugged a link off of the gear teeth. He took in several short gasps of air, then blurted out, "I need to take the bike for a test drive."

Frank studied the blueprint one last time. "Then we'll be ready for the contest." He crumbled the sketch into a ball and tossed it into the air. The crinkled paper slowly unraveled and wafted downward to the floor.

Mike snatched the flyer from the concrete. He read the heading out loud, "$50 Cash Prize to the Winner. Registration is one can of food."

"Have you ever seen fifty dollars?" Frank asked.

Mike's cheeks flushed red with excitement as he crinkled the flyer in his hand. "One of us has to win the grand prize." Mike threw the crumpled blueprint into the air.

Tom snatched the scrunched-up flyer and stuffed it into his front pants pocket. "I've got to win." Tom pointed to a calendar hung on the wall. The picture for the month of April was a jet-black Project J-38 Spyder bike. "I've been dreaming about buying this bike for months."

Frank mounted the torn leather banana seat, grabbed the ape hangers, pedaled in a circle, and stopped at the door. "What are you going to do with the Sting Ray if you buy that new bike?"

Mike mounted his fire red, hand-crafted wheelie bike and said, "I would never give the Renegade up." He flexed his biceps. "I built her with my own two hands." Slapping his right hand over his heart, Mike declared, "This bike is a part of me."

"Blue Lightning is an original, a one of a kind," Frank said. "I put a lot of hard work and sweat into finding all the parts and putting them together."

Tom walked his lime-green bike between the two boys and said, "That's the point. Our bikes are just a hodgepodge of old parts from the trash." He straddled the frame and flopped onto the seat strapped with duct tape. "People threw those bikes away because they didn't want them anymore."

"One person's trash is another person's treasure," Mike said.

"Lightning never strikes the same place twice," Frank said. "We're the only kids in town with chopped-up bikes."

"I'm talking about the Project J-38." Tom clicked the shifter into first gear. "Can you imagine what the kids at school will say when I ride a J-38 through the village?"

Tom rattled the 5-speed into third and snapped, "They'll flip out!" In his mind, he pictured the kids who'd teased him. *I might slug Bobby anyways. That goon is always starting trouble.*

The ticking of the old wall clock over the workbench grabbed their attention. The clock read 11:40 a.m.

"It's getting later by the minute. I need to win that fifty dollars," Tom said. "Let's see how this chain holds up." He threw the 5-gear shifter mounted on the main crossbar into second gear and charged down the driveway.

Mike and Frank bolted down the driveway after Tom, who threw the shifter into fourth gear, rattling the chain across the gear teeth. The chain skipped back into second gear, and the rear tire braked with a jolt. Mike and Frank zoomed passed the Sting Ray and took the lead toward Main Street.

"See ya! Wouldn't want to be ya!" Mike yelled back to his friends. His feet furiously cranked the pedals.

Tom fidgeted with the shifter, shaking and joggling it back into forth. The Sting Ray rolled into third gear, and Tom sped off.

Frank glanced back over his shoulder. "He's gaining on us!"

"Let's really test the Sting Ray's chain," Mike said. "Stomp on it. Faster. Faster!"

Chapter 2

Close Call

Preparation for the parade had begun. The village police were redirecting traffic off Main Street, while volunteers positioned barricades to detour cars from entering. An occasional tractor-trailer hauling a delivery to the neighboring state of Vermont was allowed to drive through. The early afternoon sun glared across the enormous windows of the old high school, casting its silhouette out onto the road. A hot pretzel vendor positioned her cart in the coolness of the building's shadow. A few villagers opened folding chairs near the curb, staking claims to the best seats along the parade route.

Chain Links

The chatter of the three boys echoed from around the corner of the school's limestone walls from Mechanic Street. Their bikes bumped over the curb and skidded to a stop beside a steel barrel. The glossy black paint on the metal drum glittered and sparkled in the sun.

"That's weird. I don't remember seeing this can here before," Tom said. He pushed his glasses up the bridge of his nose and read the pink words painted on the side. "Lend a hand with a can."

"Why would someone paint that on a trash can?" Mike asked.

"Hey. Hot pretzels," Frank said, pointing to the street vender. "Yummy. I love pretzels." A drop of drool rolled from the corner of his mouth to his chin. "Nothing tastes better than licking the salt off a coal-heated, crispy pretzel at a parade." He rubbed the dribble from his face and changed his mind. "Well, maybe a Creamsicle."

The thought of the combo of cool creamy vanilla and icy, thirst-quenching orange captured Mike's imagination. He licked his lips and asked, "How do they get that vanilla ice cream inside an orange popsicle?"

"I don't know, but you can bet your last nickel that I'm going to eat at least six of them before this day is over," Frank said.

Tom bucked up to the front of the banana seat, eager to profess his best-loved parade food. "My favorite is cotton candy," he said.

"I'm getting hungry," Frank said. He lurched forward. "Let's find a Creamsicle."

"Whoa, hold on," Tom said. "If my chain breaks, we'll have to get back home to my dad's tools."

Frank teetered to a stop and dropped one foot to the ground. He glanced at Tom with a silly smirk. Tom's brown, shaggy bangs hung matted and tangled over the thick rim of his glasses.

Tom blinked and squinted as he held the bike at a halt. "What's so funny?"

"How can you see where you're going?" Frank's belly jiggled beneath his T-shirt as he giggled.

Mike laughed and asked, "Who do you think you are with that crazy hair and your executive rims? Buddy Holly?"

"Yeah baby, Rock 'n' Roll…" Tom hollered. He pulled the black, blocky frames from the bridge of his nose and wiped the sweat from his head with the back of his forearm. "Buddy Holly was one of a kind." Tom rubbed the lenses dry with the bottom of his T-shirt. He squinted his two friends into focus. "He had style when he was on stage."

Mike and Frank wheeled a little closer to Tom.

Tom held his glasses before him, inspecting the lenses for any streaks or smudges. "Buddy Holly looked so cool singing Rock 'n' Roll and wearing glasses like these. You know what they say?"

Mike leaned back, resting his shoulders against the sissy bar, and asked, "What's that?"

"Great minds look alike," Tom said, standing straight as an arrow and straddling his bike with a smile. "I'm going to look so cool winning the contest wearing these glasses."

"My grandfather said it a little differently," Mike giggled while throwing a jab, thumping Tom's bicep and almost knocking the glasses from his hand. "Great minds think alike, and fools seldom differ."

14

"You look more like my neighbor's old English Sheepdog than that Rock 'n' Roll singer," Frank said with a laugh. "Barney's wooly fur covers his whole face. I don't think that dog has any eyes behind that bushy tangled mess."

Tom quickly asked, "Are you saying I look like a dog?"

"You and Barney have something in common," Frank replied. "I can't see either of your eyes behind your shaggy hair."

"That breed of dog has a double woolly coat of fur," growled Tom. "I read it in a book."

Mike leaned forward through the handlebars and barked, "Were you born wicked smart, or do you just read a lot?"

"The sheep think the dog is just another sheep and accept the dog into the flock as a friend," Tom said, holding his hands to the sides of the banana seat and shrugging his shoulders. "That's what the book said."

"You're a nerd," Frank said.

"I'm wicked smart because I read a lot," Tom snarled. "You both should try it some time."

Frank gently poked his right elbow into Mike's ribs. "Here comes another lesson," he said. "Go ahead, professor."

"You think that dog looks strange and can't see," Tom lectured from his bicycle soapbox. "It's shaggy fur and excellent eyesight keep the sheep and shepherd safe. Being different from other dogs is how it won the respect of shepherds."

Frank straightened his spine, pinched his shoulders back, and lifted his round chin. "Being the shortest in our class means I'm always first when we lineup for lunch."

Mike smiled, "Our bikes are different. I hope that difference wins the judges' respect."

"There's not another bike like ours in town," Tom said. "They're one of a kind."

"Hey, Mr. Smarty Pants. Let's finish this test ride so we can get to the competition," Mike said. "We might have a chance to win this contest, after all."

Frank straddled the banana seat and waddled his bike forward. "Hey, I got a wicked smart idea," he said, stopping. "Let's finish the test by racing up the sidewalk to the park and get a Creamsicle."

Mike stood upright and thrusted his weight down onto the pedals. The front tire of his flaming red wheelie bike jumped forward.

"Last one to the park eats a rotten egg!" Mike yelled as he sped off.

Frank threw his body backwards, thumping his shoulder blades against the sissy bar. The twelve-inch front tire bolted upward from the concrete sidewalk. "Take cover!" Frank shouted. "You're about to be struck by the Blue Lightning!"

Tom shifted his lime-green 5-speed into third gear. "Get out of the way of the Sting-Ray." He set chase, screaming, "This race is on!"

Mike caught a flicker of the Blue Lightning's extended forks from the corner of his eye, and Frank darted past the Renegade in a flash.

16

"Boom!" Frank shouted as he wildly pumped the pedals faster and faster. "You always hear thunder after lightning strikes."

Tom sped past Mike and raced up beside Frank. "Eat my dust!" he shouted, shifting into fourth gear. *Brat-a-tat-tat* rattled his chain while splattering grease onto the sidewalk.

The Blue Lightning rolled across a small glop of gunk, smearing the slimy sludge between the treads. The tire slithered slightly out of control.

Mike called on every ounce of leg strength he had left. The Renegade's red and white handgrip streamers waved as he battled back the lead. "Goodbye."

The three bikes jumped the curb and crossed Hudson Place. The police barricades prevented them from entering onto Main Street. The boys continued up the sidewalk exchanging the lead, first the Blue Lightning, and then the Renegade. Tom shifted into fifth gear and dashed into first place.

Twenty yards ahead of the race, a portly, middle-aged man exited the door of Emery's Barber Shop. The screen door swung closed and banged off the frame. The man trotted down the steps and walked onto the sidewalk.

The Sting Ray extended its lead, and Tom looked back to tease his two friends. He spotted a lone bicyclist pedaling thirty yards away. The bicyclist suddenly turned right onto Hudson Place and disappeared behind the jewelry shop on the corner.

"Hey, look where you're going!" screamed the plump man as he froze in the middle of the sidewalk.

Tom swiftly downshifted from fifth to third gear as he squeezed the front handbrake. The bike skidded to a stop. He now faced the Renegade and the Blue Lightning as they charged forward.

Tom squeezed his eyes closed and peeped, "This is going to hurt."

Chain Links

"Click! Snap! Pop!"
John W. Nassivera & Bob Bates

Well… Both hands squeezed those brakes tight
Tom's knuckles turned ghostly white
Brat-a-tat-tat rattled the chain
As the screen door banged off its frame

Well… The principal stood tight and stiff
His fingers clenched into a fist
His eyes bugged out right out of his head
Both cheeks flushed bright, bright red

Click, Clink, Snap, Snap, Clack, Clack, Pop!
Strangling down to a dead-end stop
Stranded here before it began
Looking for help to make his stand

Well… Tom's head shrink to his shoulders
His bike *Thunk-thump* like a bag of boulders
The principal grimaced in a fiery furry
Where are you boys headed in such a hurry?

Well Tom raised his chin, sucked his tongue
Knitted his brow, felt a little stung
The first rule to safety of bicycle riding
Is to stop real quick before you collide

Click, Clink, Snap, Snap, Clack, Clack, Pop!
Strangling down to a dead-end stop
Stranded here before it began
Looking for help to make his stand

Well… Are you boys prepared to pay
I need you all to show the way
Lots of luck with those crazy contraptions
Because I'll be a judge at today's competition

19

John W. Nassivera

Well Tom dropped down to his knees
Yanked and yelled should have heard him plead
The greasy chain slipped across his palms
slipped through his fingers dropped like a bomb

Click, Clink, Snap, Snap, Clack, Clack, Pop!
Strangling down to a dead-end stop
Stranded here before it began
Looking for help to make his stand
Click, Clink, Snap, Snap, Clack, Clack, Pop!
Strangling down to a dead-end stop
Stranded here before it began
Looking for help to make his stand

Chapter 3

Snap! Clack! Pop!

Mike stomped his right foot down on the pedal, slamming the brake and locking the rear tire into a skid. The tire screeched across the concrete, bouncing and jerking uncontrollably.

Frank's knuckles were ghostly white as both hands squeezed the hand brakes. The pads had clogged with slimy gooey sludge. The Blue Lightning bolted forward, and in a flash, Frank jumped from his bike.

Mike shouted, "Incoming! Prepare for impact!"

Frank rolled into somersaults and flopped to a stop. His body lied sprawled in the middle of a front lawn. The Blue Lightning veered right and smashed into a green garbage can with a loud, "Clang!" The can rumbled, *Thunk-thump-clunk-clump*. It stopped inches from crushing Frank's head.

The Renegade's rear tire jolted upwards, slammed to the pavement, and shook the bike frame to a stop. Mike sat shoulder-to-shoulder next to Tom, facing back down Main Street.

"That was wicked!" Frank yelled, sitting on the ground as he brushed dirt and grass from the front of his T-shirt.

Tom bumped Mike with his shoulder and raised his hand above his head. "Yeah, cool," he said with a smile. "Give me five."

Mike slapped Tom five. His attention was pulled from the celebration by someone peeking around the corner of the jewelry shop. Mike pointed and asked, "What's that kid doing?"

A bicycle with yellow fenders ducked behind the shop.

"Ahem!" bellowed from behind Tom.

"Where are you boys going in such a hurry?" grumbled the man standing two feet away.

Mike and Frank stared at the short, stout man. He stood tight and stiff with his fists clenched in a ball, his cheeks flushed red, and his eyes bugged out of his head. It was Mr. B, from Margret Murphy Elementary School.

Still staring at the corner, Tom whispered from the corner of his mouth, "That bike was chasing after us during the race."

"Oh man," whispered Mike. "You nearly ran over the principal."

"Didn't you three learn anything in school during Bicycle Safety Week?" Mr. B snapped. He slowly opened his fists, and his eyes settled back into his head. "The first rule to safe riding is always look where you're going."

Mike was the first to apologize. "Sorry, Mr. B."

Frank stood up and grabbed the Blue Lightning's ape hangers. "Yeah. Sorry, Mr. B."

Tom brushed his bangs from his eyes. "Sorry about that, Mr. B," he said. "We're on our way to the bike contest."

"Maybe a clean haircut will improve your eyesight and prevent you from running someone over with that crazy bike," Mr. B said. "I just finished, and there was one person after me. So, if you hurry, you can be next in line."

"Yes sir, Mr. B. That's a great idea," Frank said. "We'll get right on it."

Tom raised his chin, sucked his tongue, and said to Frank, "We don't have time. What are you—?"

Mike interrupted Tom, "Yeah, as you can see, Tom needs a haircut."

In an attempt to get Tom to agree, Mike bumped his front tire into Tom's front tire.

"Hey, I just fixed that tire," Tom said. "What do you think you're doing?"

Mike answered, puffing out his chest. "If it wasn't for your friends, your bike would still be sitting in your father's garage."

Mr. B stepped between the two boys. "Didn't you boys learn anything from your last lunch detention?"

Mike became silent and slowly turned his head toward their principal.

Mr. B shook his head at Mike. "Your two older brothers spent half of last year in lunch detention." Mr. B looked straight into Mike's eyes. "I don't think they learned a thing."

Tom stood silent as a mouse and nudged Frank's arm.

Mr. B caught notice of the poke from the corner of his eye. He knitted his brow and pulled the corners of his mouth downwards. "It's starting to look like we'll need to meet a few more times." He glanced back at Mike and said, "What did we last talk about?"

The boys became completely quiet. Sitting in the office and listening to Mr. B lecture on the art of proper behavior while all of the other kids played outside during lunch recess had been torture.

Mike looked to Frank for the answer and whispered, "Help me out. What were those letters?"

Frank shrugged his shoulders and covered his mouth with one hand. "Don't look to me." Both hands dropped open at the side of his waist. Then, he abruptly lurched forward, clutched Mike's shoulders, and shouted, "I remember. The ABCs of friendship."

"The ARC of friendship: Accept, Respect, and Collaborate," Tom said, stepping forward.

Frank gave Tom a dismissive wave and said, "I was close, just one letter off."

Tom shook his head in disagreement. His bangs swung back-and-forth across his forehead like the grass skirt of a hula dancer.

Mike laughed. "Come on, Shaggy. Let's get your hair cut before you run someone over."

"Great idea," Mr. B said. "Now, are you boys prepared to pay the entry fee? Every contestant is required to donate one can of food to Doreen's Soup Kitchen & Food Pantry." Mr. B pointed at the boys. "I'm depending on you three sixth graders to represent our school."

24

"Sure thing. We got it covered, Mr. B," Mike said.

"I have to get to Paris Park and help set up the Bazaar," Mr. B said. "Oh, by the way, I'll be one of the three judges. Good luck with those crazy contraptions you call bicycles."

Mr. B turned and quickly started to walk up Main Street. He crossed Pearl Street and yelled back, "Pick up that can and the mess you made. We want to keep our community litter-free." He continued past the post office toward the courthouse.

"These bikes are different! They're bikes of the future!" Tom shouted at the back of Mr. B's head. "I'm going to get my haircut right now."

Mr. B never looked back. The boys dropped their heads and huddled around the trash can lying on its side.

Tom turned to Mike and said, "I hope Mr. B forgives us for almost running him over. Do you think he'll hold it against us?" He then slouched down, grasping the rim of the metal can, and muttered, "I really need to win that contest."

Mike stooped over the metal garbage can and said, "You better get your haircut so that when Mr. B sees you at the judging, he thinks you're respectful. Otherwise, it could be bad for all three of us."

The two boys lifted the can upright as Frank gathered the debris littered across the ground. Frank walked over to the metal container, clutching a dozen cans to his chest. The cans thumped, clunked, and thudded to the bottom of the green trash can.

"Well, that's done," Frank said. He rubbed his palms together. "The street is clean of litter. That should make Mr. B happy."

John W. Nassivera

Frank straddled the banana seat of his bike and asked, "What are we going to do about getting three cans of food for our registration?"

"I can't help," Tom said with his head sinking into his shoulders. "My dad doesn't get paid until next week, so there is nothing extra in the house."

"I can get three cans of creamed corn from my mom's pantry," Mike said. "My brothers and sister hate that soupy slime. No one will miss that barf."

The siren above the fire station four blocks away blasted its daily noon bellow out over the village, *Hhhrrrrrrnnnnngggg.*

"We better hurry!" Frank shouted over the siren. "It's noon."

The boys raced onto the lawn of Emery's barber shop. The chain rattled and clanked across the metal teeth of the gears, louder and louder.

Frank said, gasping for breath, "How are we going to get his haircut, huuuff... grab three cans of food, hisss... fix his chain, huuuff... and ride to Paris Park, hisss... huuuff... to register for the contest in time?"

"If Tom shows up to the contest without a haircut, Mr. B will be furious." Mike slowly waved his thumb like a knife across his throat. "It will be curtains for all three of us."

"Worse than that..." Frank gasped again. "We could be sentenced to a week of lunch detention."

Click, Clink, Snap, Clack, Pop! The chain snapped, skipped across the metal teeth, tumbled off the back gear, and became tangled around the pedal. The steel knot strangled the bicycle, bringing it to a halt.

26

Chapter 4

Blue Goo

Tom dropped to his knees. The greasy chain slithered across his palms and slipped through his fingers as he yanked and pulled.

"Come on, guys. Help me fix this," Tom begged.

The barber, Buck, walked out of the shop to the edge of the porch, wearing a grey barber coat. The triangular knot of a black tie laid tightly tucked beneath the corners of a white-collar shirt. His muddy, brown eyes were magnified ten times behind the horn-rimmed Coke bottle glasses.

Tom continued to wrestle with the chain, but the tangled mess only became tighter with each pull and yank.

Frank lightly jabbed his knee into Tom's shoulder and giggled under his breath, "Who's the real Buddy Holly?"

Tom stood and glanced over at Buck's bottle-thick, horn-rimmed glasses. He elbowed Frank in the upper arm and mumbled, "Real funny." Tom dropped to his knees and continued the scuffle to untangle the knotted muddle.

Buck reached over the steps and pointed out toward the street. "You boys look like you need a haircut," he bellowed across the lawn. The clicking and clinking of scissors snipped through the air.

Mike rubbed his hand over the bristles of his fresh crew cut. "I was just here with my dad three days ago."

Buck pointed his scissors at the broken chain in Tom's hands and said, "Well, you aren't going anywhere." The wooden floor planks creaked under each step as he plodded back into the shop.

Mike and Frank hovered over Tom's head, collapsing downward and pressing to take a turn.

"Hey." Mike sprung upward and modelled his Mr. Universe front double bicep pose. His upper arms puffed out from beneath the sleeves. "Why don't you let a real man take a try?" He blew a kiss to his inflated arms.

Tom fell back onto his butt and said, "Be my guest."

Mike tugged, pulled, and jimmied at the chain knot. Blood pumped through his shoulders, chest, and arms with each yank and jerk. His upper body inflated like that of a strongman in the circus.

"This isn't gonna work," Mike said, wearing a scowl. He flopped down next to Tom in defeat.

Tom's cheeks flushed red, and his brown eyes glared into his greased-covered hands. "This is a nightmare," he whimpered. "I'm doomed." Tom's head drooped to the ground. "You two go to the contest without me."

"Maybe Buck has some tools in his shop," Frank said. He grunted and heaved upward, yanked side-to-side, and jerked the greasy chain downward. He dropped the chain and pointed toward the door, saying, "Let's go ask."

Tom waved both hands across the blades of grass, smudging the grease from his palms, and jumped to his feet. "Good idea!"

Frank pointed to his head, smiled at Mike, and said, "The brain is the strongest muscle in the human body."

"Cross your fingers," Tom said, sprinting across the lawn. "Follow me."

The boys raced onto the porch and through the door before skidding to a stop in the shop. The noon sun shined through a single large picture window that looked out across the front porch onto Main Street. "Emery's" was scrolled across the top half of the glass. A single barber chair rested dead center, facing a huge wall mirror that ran the length of the shop.

"I hope that man in the chair is almost done," Mike said.

The back of the chair concealed all of the man's features, except for his brown hair hanging down over the collar of the barber's bib onto his shoulders. Buck was bent over the front of the customer, cutting away like a surgeon. Hearing the boys' babble, he stood up from his work, looked back, and said, "So, you decided to get a cut."

Mike took a step and said, "Well, not me, but my friend Tom needs something done with his hair."

A cheerful voice from the chair spoke up, "Looks cool. Thanks, man."

Buck whispered with a lighthearted smile down at the man. "I hardly cut a hair."

"You're like the Leonardo da Vinci of barbers," said the customer. "This cut is a work of art."

The boys stared at his reflection in the mirror. The man, who was in his early twenties, parted his hair down the middle of his forehead and tucked his flowing bangs over his earlobes. Thin, wire-framed glasses were perched on the nose of his slim face. He pulled a denim jacket from the coatrack and threw it over his shoulders. The customer grasped the handle of a tattered guitar case from the floor and faced the boys.

"It looks like you boys are in a hurry," he said. "Well, I've got to get to the Music Hall and practice with the band for this evening's concert in the park. I hope to see you dudes at our gig tonight."

The screen door swung open as the musician called back, "People who sing together, come together." The door clacked against the frame twice as it shut, and the musician's voice rang out, "People Power!"

Frank gazed in awe at the screen door before slowly turning to Mike with an open mouth. "He's that Rock 'n' Roll singer that started the Music Hall on Maple Street," Frank said. "My older sister takes drum lessons there for free."

"Did you see the peace sign on his jacket?" asked Mike. "I've never seen a guy that cool before."

"I can't wait for the concert tonight," Frank said. "My sister said the band is going to play all the latest and greatest Rock 'n' Roll hits."

"Come on, get a grip, guys." Tom grabbed the two friends by their arms. "We're here for tools, not an autograph."

At that moment, an aromatic whisk of mint tingled the boys' nostrils. Frank swiftly pinched his nose closed. Mike gagged, and Tom sneezed an explosive shriek. They tracked the scent across the room to the mirror. Buck held the silver top off a tall glass jar and dipped his black comb into a blue goo. The smell became more potent with each dipping.

Buck turned to the boys and asked, "Which one of you is Tom?"

The boys all let out an ear-splitting, "Achoo!"

Buck swiveled the chair in a circle and said, "Now, make like a deer and leap up into this chair."

Tom pinched his nose to ward off another sneeze and said with a nasal tone, "Sir, do you have any tool…achoo!"

Buck said, "Let's put a fire under your feet and jump into the seat. I don't have a lot of time. I'm closing early today so I can clean up for the parade."

Tom glanced around the barber shop as he slowly climbed into the chair. There was no toolbox in sight.

Buck took a step back from the chair, stood at attention, and pointed to a portrait of a young marine hanging to the left of the mirror. "That handsome soldier sporting a crew cut in his military dress uniform is my son. He's currently serving in the Vietnam War. Do you want a haircut like his?"

"You must be proud to have a son who's a hero," Frank said. "When is he coming home?"

Buck said, "He's twenty-eight years old and has always been my hero." His clown-like smile suddenly fell to a frown. "I know my three

31

grandchildren and his wife miss him dearly." Buck dropped his hands to his sides, and the shop became silent.

Tom limply slouched into the leather seat and glanced under the counter in search of a toolbox.

"It's very hard not having a husband and dad at home," Buck said. "Maggie struggles to pay the rent, put enough food on the table, and keep clothing in my grandchildren's closets." Buck stared at his reflection in the mirror and softly said, "I try to help as much as I can, but it just isn't enough."

"Maybe the village will have a parade like today when your son returns," Mike said.

Buck stood tall with his chin up, chest out, shoulders back, and stomach in, saying, "All our young men and women fighting for our country deserve a parade." He then returned his attention to Tom. "So, how would you like your hair cut today?"

Tom looked to the door. "I'm trying to grow my hair long, like the customer who just left."

"What's going on with young people?" Buck asked. "If this long hair style continues, nobody will need a haircut. I'll be out of business."

"Sorry, sir, but we really came to ask if you had some tools we could borrow to fix my bike," Tom said. "It's just that my bicycle chain broke, and I need help to fix it."

Buck silently stepped to the mirror, meticulously combed his hair, and vainly admired his reflection. The comb plopped into the blue goo. He struts across the room and squinted out the front window. Paradegoers began to sit on the sidewalk by the street curb. "The good seats are going fast." Buck slid

32

his coat sleeve above his wrist and glanced at his watch. "There's less than two hours before the parade starts."

Tom jumped up out of the chair. "I have to get my bike fixed," he shouted.

Buck pointed at Mike. "Go check the closet for my toolbox and grab the broom while you're in there."

Mike took several steps to his left, opened the door, and disappeared. "I can't see a thing," he cried out from the darkness. "Where's the light switch?"

Buck reached in and pulled a string that hung from the ceiling right in front of Mike's nose. A bright light beamed through the small closet.

Mike walked out of the closet, blinking his eyes and holding the broom in his right hand. "There's no toolbox, sir."

Buck grabbed the broom and handed it to Tom. "Sweep all that hair into a pile," he ordered.

"Sir, I don't mean any disrespect, but I need to fix my bike right now," Tom said.

Buck removed his barber coat, laid it across the chair, and turned back to his reflection in the mirror. He tugged and pinched the knot of his tie.

"Sir?" Tom said.

"Just give me a minute to remember where those tools are," Buck said. He unfolded his right shirt sleeve to his wrist and buttoned it closed. Buck's reflection pivoted to his right as he began to sing, "What would you do if hmm, hmm, hmm…"

Without delay, Tom swept the hair on the floor into a pile. He called out over Buck's humming, "Excuse me, sir. Has the location of your tools come to mind yet?"

"I can't get this tune out of my head," Buck said. "That young musician sang this song he plans to sing tonight." Buck's fingertips rubbed and kneaded the side of his head, joggling his eyes in their sockets as he said, "It just won't leave my head."

"Mr. Buck, do you remember where your toolbox is?" Tom asked.

He stopped in the middle of the floor and rubbed his chin. "Now, where did I last use that toolbox? Maybe it's in the storage closet."

Tom stepped behind Buck as he opened the door. The room was small, approximately five feet by ten feet. It was dark, dingy, and filled wall-to-wall with junk.

"I think the toolbox is in here somewhere." Buck pointed, "Hey, take a look over there, past that pile of junk."

A discarded watchman's chair was propped against a heap of cardboard boxes. Wedged between the wall and top row of boxes was an old hall tree.

"How can I see anything with this pile of stuff in the way?" Tom asked.

Buck pushed his glasses up the bridge of his nose. "Just climb up on that chair and take a look around. Don't worry about breaking anything. It's all junk."

Tom cautiously climbed onto the seat and stood on his tiptoes, unable to see over the top row of boxes. He grasped a branch of the hall tree, carefully pulled upward, and peered out over the top row. Stacks upon stacks of boxes piled side-to-side stretched across the room to the far wall.

"No toolbox over here, sir," Tom said.

"Climb down from there before you hurt yourself." Buck walked out of the closet and said, "I just remembered where I last used my tools."

A deafening silence hovered over the shop. Tom felt a heaviness on his shoulders as the hair on the back of his neck stood up. His heart began to jitter, and his body shivered into a cold sweat. "Hey, where are Mike and Frank?"

Buck pointed toward the barber chair. The lid laid beside the jar of goo on the counter. Above, a slimy blue message was smudged across the mirror, which read, "Running out of time."

John W. Nassivera

"Don't Stop"
John W. Nassivera & Bob Bates

Clinking of scissors snipped through the air
Slumped into a crouch on the barber's chair
Rubbing the bristles of fresh crew cut hair
If you remember, we might have a prayer

Buck's fingertips rubbed his head
Humming a tune loud enough to wake the dead
Joggling his eyes in their sockets he said
The tools are in the garage past my shed

A rusty hasp strapped two hulking locks
An iron shank jammed the heart-shape padlock
Rub a penny in his pocket
He dashed inside like a speeding rocket

His cheeks flushed pale pink to bright cherry red
The corners of his mouth raised towards his head
Colson and Norman the bike tags read
Schwinn Starlet and Panther, he raced ahead

Unusual frames, rare seats, quirky lights
The strangest-looking two-wheeled bikes in sight
Admiring my first tool, feeling strength and might
The chain is together, things are looking bright

Tom circled back skidded to a stop
From a radio the size of a shoe box
A gritty wolf howl, a DJ shouts bop
The parade is about to start, so don't stop
The parade is about to start, so don't stop
The parade is about to start, you've got a shot

Chapter 5

The Fix

The back of Tom's ears flushed red. His jaw clenched shut, grinding and gnashing his teeth. He cried out, "I'll never make it in time!"

"Hey, I just remembered. I left the toolbox in the garage," Buck said. "Come with me."

A rusty, metal latch strapped two hulking, weathered garage doors shut. Buck pulled a key from his pants pocket and firmly grasped the heart-shaped steel padlock. He jammed the iron shank into the rusty keyway. After several clinks, the rust-pitted shackle popped upward, releasing the padlock from the door latch.

"I keep all my valuable junk in the garage," Buck said.

The sunlight crept into the cavernous bay as the two slowly pulled the doors open. Tom staggered to a stopped and tucked a hand tightly into the front pocket of his faded blue jeans. He fidgeted with his lucky penny, rubbing the tip of his index finger over Lincoln's raised head.

Buck stood tall, straight as an arrow, and dropped his hand on Tom's shoulder. He whooped with delight, "So, what do you think?"

Tom broke his stare at the ground and slowly raised his head.

"WOW!" Tom's mouth dropped wide open, and his weight fell back on his heels.

The two-car garage was filled three rows deep with old bikes of every color imaginable. There were even colors Tom had only read about, like smaragdine, falu, and fuzzy wuzzy brown. One bike had two handlebars and two seats. It was built for two people to ride at the same time.

Tom jumped into the garage and giddily swayed back-and-forth in front of the twin bike. His cheeks flushed from pale pink to bright cherry red, and the corners of his mouth raised towards the top of his head.

"I've read about bikes made for two people, but I never saw one."

Buck chuckled and said, "You think that's unique? Look over to your left against the wall."

Tom quickly turned and spotted a bike with one wheel and no handlebars. "It's a unicycle." Tom lifted the seat perched on a single wheel and giddily asked, "How do you steer this thing?"

"Come over here," Buck said, waving to Tom from the back of the garage. "Let me show you my pride and joy."

A dusty cloth tarp draped from the ceiling rafters above the second-floor loft to the dirt floor.

"Close your eyes, and count to three."

Tom closed his eyes and began to count, "One."

He paused, clenching his hands into fists to subdue the anticipation. Suspense shivered down his spine.

"Two," Tom called out. "Three."

Buck released his grip, and the tarp dropped with a clatter and hit the ground with a hefty thwack. Tom leaned back and gaped at the seat standing ten feet above the ground.

"Whoa! Far out! What do you call it?" He bounced forward and rollicked around the sky-high two-wheeler. "How do you get up onto the seat? Can you really ride that thing?"

"It's called a Penny-farthing," Buck said, pointing to a wooden ladder that rose from the floor up into the second story. "You have to climb this twelve-foot stepladder to get onto the seat. And yes, people can ride it."

Tom shook his head in amazement. "Can you show me?"

"It's been a good twenty to thirty years since I last rode her." Buck scratched his chin, and his eyes climbed up the frame to the seat. "I'm getting older. I'm not sure if I still have what it takes to ride her anymore."

"That's crazy cool." Tom pointed to the rafters. "It's not like any bicycle I've ever read about."

"Yeah, she's a beauty," Buck said with a silly grin on his face. "The toolbox is over on the workbench." He took several steps and waved Tom toward the doors. "Go get your bike from the front of the shop." Buck flopped down on a stool and opened the steel box. "I'm sure we can fix the chain."

Tom sprinted down the driveway and disappeared around the corner of the house. He returned to the garage with the Sting Ray by his side and zig-zagged between a 1930s Colson Flyer and a 1955 Norman. He studied the bikes in the first two rows.

"Schwinn Starlet, Schwinn Panther, Schwinn Hornet, Schwinn Varsity, Schwinn World Traveler," Tom read from their nametags out loud as he passed. "Hey, I guess you like Schwinn."

Buck sat on a stool at the workbench, tinkering with a tool. Without looking up, he said, "Yeah, I fell in love with Schwinn when I got my first tricycle at the age of three on Christmas."

Tom strolled past the bikes, admiring unusual frames, rare seats, and quirky headlights along the way. He thought to himself, *Wow! Buck has had bikes since he was three years old. The Sting Ray is my first bike.*

"This is the first time that a bike like yours has been in the garage." Buck bent forward from the stool. "It's the strangest-looking two-wheel contraption I have ever seen," Buck said, turning back to the benchtop and shuffling through the toolbox. "Now that I think of it, no two bikes in here are the same." He looked back over his shoulder and surveyed the rows of bikes. "Your bike is going to fit right in."

Tom flipped the kickstand down and stepped away from his bike.

"So, what's the lowdown on this bike?" Buck asked.

Tom shrugged and lifted both hands out to his sides. "What do you mean?"

40

"Tell me about your bike, son." Buck eyes were glued on the toolbox.

"Some kids call this bike style a wheelie bike, or a banana bike, or a Spyder bike," Tom said. "Have you ever heard about a guy named Al Fritz? He designs bikes for some big bike company."

Buck immediately stopped searching through the toolbox and focused his attention on Tom.

Tom paused, surprised by Buck's sudden curiosity.

"Anyways, some kids in California had built bikes with old parts that made them look like chopper motorcycles," Tom said. "Fritz liked the style so much, he designed Project J-38. Every kid my age wants one." He glanced from Buck to the Sting Ray. "Project J-38s cost too much money, exactly fifty dollars, so me and my friends built our own wheelie bikes."

Buck rubbed his chin and said, "It sounds like you did your research."

"Yeah, I like to read." Tom pulled his glasses from his face and cleaned the lenses with the bottom of his shirt.

"People respect a smart, hard-working person," Buck said.

"Thank you, sir," Tom said. "I hope it pays off by me winning the fifty dollars first prize. I really want the J-38."

Buck stood up from the stool and walked around Tom's bike. He pulled upward on the sissy bar, sat on the banana seat with his arms draped from the ape hangers, and even measured the length of the front forks.

"I felt there was something familiar about your bike. Did you know that Al Fritz is a designer for Schwinn?"

"No, sir. I don't think I've read that."

"I also read a lot," Buck said as he inspected the long, extended front forks a second time. He stepped to the back of the bike and grinned as he eyed the long, slender banana shaped seat. "Well, I read about bikes a lot. So, let's see if we can fix yours."

Tom bent down on one knee and tugged on the chain. "The chain was too loose, and now, I've got a broken link."

"I have just the tool. It's called a chain breaker." Buck lifted a metal drawer from his toolbox. "Here it is." Buck's hand was closed in a fist. "Flip your bike upside down. Time for some surgery."

Tom flipped his bike onto its seat and handlebars. Buck pried the tangled chain from the pedal with a screwdriver and laid it across the workbench.

"Now, the trick is to remove two links so that both ends of the chain will link together properly," Buck said. He laid the chain breaker next to the broken link.

Tom grasped the breaker between his index finger and thumb. "Can I give it a try?" Tom asked.

"Sure. Just rest the broken chain link across the two posts and crank down on the rivet."

Tom tentatively turned the breaker. Suddenly there were several clicks, and then a loud pop. The rivet dropped to the benchtop. His voice trembled, "Did I break it?"

"It was broken before you started," Buck said with a smile.

Tom smiled with relief.

"What's next?" Tom asked, having cautiously did everything Buck asked him to do.

"There it is. Your chain is back together, stronger than ever," Buck said. He clapped his hands together, smiled, and said, "Slip it over the gears and give it a try."

Tom slid the chain over the jagged steel teeth and slowly spun the pedal. The chain clicked and clanked before it clunked onto the gears. Tom grabbed the chain between his thumb and index finger and pulled upward, and the chain clung tight to the gear teeth.

"Are you going to see how she rides?" Buck asked.

Tom flipped the bike upright, jumped onto the banana seat, darted out of the garage, and zoomed down the driveway. He circled back and skidded to a stop in front of the doors. Buck sat in the back of the garage, tinkering with the tuner on an old wooden AM radio the size of a shoe box. A loud, scratchy noise crackled and hissed from a single small speaker the size of a softball.

"Perfect," Tom said as he pushed his bike toward the back of the garage. "Never better. Now I have a chance to win first prize and buy that new bike. Thanks, Buck."

"Every link needs to do its job for the chain to hold together," Buck fidgeted with the nob to the right of the speaker.

Buck's eyes remained fixated on the knob as he slowly turned it to the left. A voice came over the speaker and then quickly faded back to static.

"How much money did you say first prize was?" Buck asked.

"Fifty dollars," Tom said.

"That gives me an idea." Buck turned the radio knob in a complete circle and stopped. "I wonder if my daughter-in-law would be interested in my plan."

"Maybe I can help with the radio," Tom said.

"Hey, catch," called out Buck as he tossed the breaker into the air.

"Wow! I can keep it?" Tom asked as he caught the breaker. "For real?"

"Yeah," Buck said.

"This is my first tool," he said, admiring the piece of iron. He reached behind him and tucked it deep into his back pocket. "Thanks, Buck."

"You're welcome. Make sure to put it to good use." Buck shuffled out the garage doors and waddled up several steps onto the back porch. "I've got to make that phone call," Buck said before disappearing into the shop.

Tom turned his attention back to the radio. He twitched the nob to the left and clicked it back to the right.

"ARH-WOOOOOOOOOOOO!" A long, loud wolf howl blasted from the small speaker. Then, the gravelly, deep voice of a radio jockey announced, "If you're not at the park, you'll be left out in the dark. You have less than one hour before you miss the parade of the year."

Chapter 6

A Race Against Time

Tom raced down the driveway. The sidewalk was packed eight rows back from the street with people of all ages waiting for the start of the parade. He squeezed both hand brakes and skidded to a stop, inches from the heels of a father with his two-year-old son perched on his shoulders. Tom jumped to the ground and walked his bike uptown behind the human wall of paradegoers, searching for a safe opening.

At the corner of Pearl Street and Main Street, the gathering of spectators created a roadblock that stretched from the street curb, across the sidewalk, and up the stairs to the front doors of the post office. The monumental town clock towered majestically above the crowd one block away. The long, thin hand was pointed to the number six, and the stubby hand laid between the two and three.

Tom swiveled away from the crowd and glanced down Pearl Street in search of an escape route. Three women straggled up the sidewalk towards Main Street, one pushing a young child in a stroller. They gaggled and dilly-dallied in the shade beneath the tall oaks beside the post office.

"Look at this crowd. Every man, woman, and child living in the village must be at this parade," one of the stragglers said as she moseyed past Tom.

A second straggler groaned at the sight and said, "Yeah, I didn't see one person on Mulberry or Cherry Street." The three ambled to a halt behind the crowd.

"That's it!" Tom shouted as he sped off down Pearl Street away from the parade route. He released the right handgrip and shifted gears, boosting his speed. Fifty yards down the road, he leaned out from the banana seat, dipping the bike and banking tight into a left turn onto Mulberry Street. The pedal scraped the blacktop, shaking the bike frame. Tom instantly shifted his body over the seat, leveling the bike upright.

An old rust bucket of a pickup truck turned onto Mulberry. Its engine knocked and popped a puff of grey smoke from under the hood as the truck trudged down the street.

Tom stood upright on the pedals, dropped his head, pumped his thighs with all his might, and dashed up the middle of the road.

The old engine hissed, growled, and roared through its jagged radiator grille as the truck charged forward. Its monstrous chassis shuddered and trembled over the four tires as it gained speed, heading straight for Tom.

Tom lifted his head and found himself staring straight into the blinking round headlights of the massive truck.

46

Chain Links

Aaht aahht beeeeeep! honked the driver.

Tom dropped down onto the seat and cranked the handlebars to the left. The bike veered from the middle of the road as the harsh screech of the truck brakes pierced his ears. Tom jumped the street curb as the corner of the truck's front bumper missed the treads of the Sting Ray's rear mag tire by a fraction of an inch. The curb jolted the bike upward, bucking Tom from the banana seat like a wild bronco. He plummeted to the grass, tumbled across the front lawn, and rolled to a stop, flat on his back.

His eyes opened to a gargantuan hand with portly sausage-shaped fingers extending from a callous palm. A massive body connected to the hand cast a dark shadow over Tom's face. The truck driver's enormous paw clamped around Tom's bicep and lifted him to his feet.

"Are you okay?" asked the truck driver.

Tom shook the cobwebs from his head and moaned, "Yeah." His eyes suddenly bugged out of his head, and he shrieked, "Where's my bike?" He bobbed his head to the left and bounced back to the right. "Is it okay?"

The driver squinted from under his bushy eyebrows and a tattered baseball cap. The bristly grey hairs of his mustache sprouted every which way like the quills on a porcupine's back, completely covering his top lip.

"Do you know you were riding the wrong way down a one-way street?" asked the driver in a gruff, gravelly voice.

"I was rushing to make it to the bike contest in time." Tom's lower lip twitched, his brown eyes fluttered, and he stuttered, "I didn't see a one-way sign."

The monstrous man took one step to his left, reveling a steel pole rising ten feet above the ground. On top was a black and white street sign that read "One-Way."

"See that white arrow pointing down the street?"

Tom bowed his head and said, "Sorry, sir."

"Your bike is fine. Not a scratch," the driver said. He turned and pointed to the bed of the pickup truck. The Sting Ray leaned up against the back bumper.

"Do you know what time it is, sir?" Tom ran to his bike and mounted.

The man bent down and stuck his head into the cab through the passenger window. His voice bellowed out the rear slide window. "The clock on the dashboard reads 2:45."

"I'll never make it to Paris Park in time." Tom jumped from the bike and slapped the rusted back fender of the truck in anger. The Sting Ray fell to the ground with a clunk.

The truck driver pulled his head back and stepped to the rear of his truck.

"I'm sorry, sir," Tom whimpered. A shiver ran up his spine as his mouth dropped wide open. "I didn't do any damage to your truck." He bent over and rubbed both hands in circles over the fender. "Look, not a scratch in the rust anywhere."

The enormous burly man reached out with his beefy arm. Tom stepped back and cowered against the side of the truck. The driver grasped the Sting Ray in one hand and lifted the bike above Tom's head.

However, to Tom's relief, the man gently dropped the bike into the bed of the truck. His whole body wiggled and wobbled as he strode to the driver side door.

"Get in," the truck driver said. He shimmied across the seat, jiggling and joggling his big, round belly behind the steering wheel. His large, plump hand hid the key from sight as he reached behind the wheel and turned the ignition. A knock and then a pop of grey smoke rolled from under the hood as the engine roared.

Tom raced from the back of the truck to the passenger side and leaped up onto the raggedy bench seat. The truck jerked from the curb, and the door slammed shut.

They groaned along Maple, rolled up Center Street past the Bowling Alley, and chugged toward the gates of Paris Park. The engine rumbled to a stop on Locust Street, and the driver exited the cab. Tom leaped from the seat to the street. He ran down the side of the truck to the back bumper, finding the truck driver with the Sting Ray in his hand.

"Here you go, son," the truck driver said, wearing an enormous smile. "When you wear a smile, you brighten everyone's day. See you in the parade."

Tom grabbed the bike from the man and raced to the gate. He stopped, turned back, and yelled, "Thank you for the ride! It means so much to me to be in this contest."

The man shimmied into his truck and slammed the door. His hefty arm flopped out the window and slapped the door panel. Flakes of rust and white paint splintered and fell to the road. Tom struggled to read the painted white words on the truck. The paint had faded under a green and brown film of rust.

Wearing a clown-like smile, the driver yelled over the rumbling engine, "Good Luck!"

The truck drove off, rattling and banging puffs of black smoke from under its hood.

The field in front of Tom was chaotic with crews setting up the food court and craft stands. Volunteer workers had brought in the carnival rides for the night's bazaar. More than fifty bicycles parked in rows of ten crowded the far corner of the field. Tom rushed toward a tall, thin woman, who stood guard at the gate with a clipboard hugging close to her blouse.

A chain of safety pins dangled from the spring clip as the lanky woman's spindly arms waved him to a stop. She shuffled several papers, clasped them to the board without making eye contact, and said, "Name and entry number, please."

Out of breath, Tom wheezed, "My name is..." He took a deep, long gasp, expanding his chest and ribs, and continued, "Tom, but I don't have an entry number."

The woman held her hand open inches in front of Tom's face, blocking his view of the stage. She slowly pulled her hand back, looked at her wristwatch, and pointed off to the side.

"The registration table is over there," she said. "You better run like your life depends on it."

"Rules Are Rules"
John W. Nassivera & Bob Bates

Well... an old rusty truck, growled and reared
Monstrous engine, striking fear
Tom flopped on the ground, a bruise on his crown
A big burly man, reached right down
Lifted him up, to the seat
Then chugged-a log, and raced up the street

Time was almost gone, a lady waved him on
Pumping and a flailing, Tom was really gone
Register please, the man wants a can
With no can in hand, your bicycle is banned
Step out of line, let everybody through
It's the same everywhere, man rules are the rules

Rules are rules, man that's always fair
Rules are rules, don't you be no square
Sorry to say it's the way it rolls
Settle down, you can reach your goal
Rules are rules, that's where it's at
Rules are rules, you'll get your turn at bat

Well... Heart pounding right, out of Tom's chest
Register for three, but I've done my best
Sixty-eight, sixty-nine, seventy is mine
Cheeks clung to Tom's teeth, feeling mighty fine
Not a second there, is to spare, raced to the end with a boyish flair

Rules are rules, worked out for the better
Rules are rules, came down to the last letter
Standing at the stage, it's so cool
We are number one, we're nobody's fool
Rules are rules, man its where it's at
Rules are rules, got my turn at bate
Well...

John W. Nassivera

Rules are rules, worked out for the better
Rules are rules, came down to the last letter
Standing at the stage, it's so cool
We are number one, we're nobody's fool
Rules are rules, man its where it's at
Rules are rules, got my turn at bate

Chapter 7

Rules Are Rules

Tom dropped his bike to the ground and bolted into a sprint. Legs pumping and arms flailing, he dashed to the table in three seconds flat. He flopped downward, his heart pounding the top of the table through his chest.

An old, bald man sat in a folding chair and flipped through a stack of registration forms resting on his lap. His eyebrows lifted and gave a fleeting glimpse at Tom collapsed over the table. "May I help you, son?" the registrar asked as he continued to inspect the forms.

"Yes," Tom gasped, lifting his sweaty head.

The man slowly heaved the stack from his lap, dropped the pile, and grasped the tabletop. The knobby knuckles of eight bony fingers flushed a pale bluish gray as a pair of scrawny legs pushed his rickety body upright. He moaned and said, "Your entry fee, please."

Tom dropped his head, bumping it off the tabletop twice. Mr. B's voice echoed inside his skull; *I want you sixth graders to make me proud.* Tom slowly stood, folded both hands in front of his chest, and said to the man across the table, "I'm sorry, but my bike broke down, and I didn't have time."

The old man's arms trembled to support his weight. His thin eyebrows quivered on top of his stern brow as he glanced downward at his wristwatch. "You have ten minutes." The man's right hand slapped down on top of the stack. "You better hurry if you want to enter your bike in the contest."

"There's no way." Tom's hands began to twitch, and his bottom lip quivered. "My dad doesn't get paid for a week. There's no extra food at home."

"Sorry son, but the rules are the rules," the registrar said. He pulled the registration forms from the table, flopped atop the chair, and flipped through the stack.

Tom dropped his head, kicked at the ground, and muttered, "I did all this work for nothing." He clenched both hands into fists and felt his body stiffen from his head to his toes.

"What are those punks at school going to think of me now?" His shoulders tensed, his lower lip trembled, and he stammered, "I don't care what mom said. I'm going to punch Bobby right in the face if he says one word."

"Move out of the way, young man." The old man waved Tom off the line. "We still have people trying to register."

"I can't believe this." Tom turned toward the exit. The weight of disappointment held him still, as though he was standing in a bucket of concrete. "If those kids say one thing about my bike on Monday, I swear I'll knock them all out." He dragged his body several steps to the end of the table and mumbled, "Why couldn't my dad have gotten paid yesterday?"

Four hands dropped three cans onto the table.

"Registrations for three," said the next person in line.

"Three? I only see two of you," the registrar said. "Your friend better hurry. I'm closing the registration in six minutes."

Tom stood stiff as a board, clenching both hands into fists.

54

The registrar slid a blank form to the end of the table. His pale hands quivered as he dropped a pencil next to it.

In a voice a little more than a murmur, Tom said, "Are you crazy? You just told me to get off the line."

"Are you going to register, or are you going to stand there talking to yourself?" the old man asked.

Tom glanced up.

Mike and Frank stood shoulder-to-shoulder beside the table and laughed. Tom charged forward. The two boys tee-heed and giggled. Tom pounced onto their backs.

"You guys are the best!" Tom shouted.

The three jumped for joy within each other's arms, frolicking and prancing in a circle.

The registrar interrupted the boy's celebration, saying, "You boys may want to stop playing Ring Around the Rosie. You only have five minutes to get through that gate, and I need my paperwork before you can leave."

The boys rushed up to the table, grabbed pencils, and began to frantically scribble their full names and addresses on the forms.

The old man slowly rubbed the sides of his head. His long forehead rose, and wrinkles rippled across the top of his bald head. "Print the required information so I can read it," he said.

Frank wrote his zip code. All he had left was to sign his name. He took a quick glance at the other boys' forms. Mike was a zip code and signature away from completing his registration. Frank raced to scribble his signature as Mike scrawled the first number of the zip code. Frank hastily slid his form across the table to finish first. Mike finished in a lickety-split and passed his registration across the table.

The man silently read, paying pain-staking attention to each piece of information written on the two boys' registration forms. He placed the forms on top of the paper pile and slid the boys' entry numbers across the table, saying, "Number sixty-eight and number sixty-nine."

Tom's right hand began to cramp around the pencil. He crossed the letter "T" and dotted his "i's." The pencil dropped to the table, and he passed the form to the man.

The registrar tediously inspected the form. Tom nervously looked over his shoulder to the woman at the gate. She was staring down at her wristwatch and tapping her left foot on the ground.

"Is something wrong?" Tom asked.

"Entry number seventy," the man said as he slid the paper across the table. "Please proceed to the gate and present your entry numbers."

They ran to the gate and handed their entry numbers to the woman. She turned to the last page on her clipboard and, in a snappy tone of voice, asked, "Your names?"

The boys hurriedly answered at the same time, "Frank. Mike. Tom."

She scratched three check marks on a paper attached to the clipboard and commanded, "Present your bikes, please."

Frank wheeled his bike to the gate and stated, "Blue Lightning."

In a sharp, explosive tone, the gate keeper asked, "Type of bicycle?"

"Banana bike," Frank swiftly answered.

Chain Links

She unhooked two small safety pins from the dangling hoop attached to the clipboard and pinned the official entry number on the front of his shirt, saying, "Proceed."

Mike rolled his bike forward to the gate. "Renegade. It's a wheelie bike."

The woman pined the entry number to the front of his shirt and directed him through the gate.

The inside walls of Tom's cheeks clung to the sides of his teeth. His lips parted with a smack. "Sting Ray," Tom croaked. "It's a Spyder bike."

The woman stared down at her wristwatch, not saying a word.

John W. Nassivera

"Stick to the Plan"
John W. Nassivera & Bob Bates

Left you a slimy clue, hands stink with blue goo
Without any cans to pay, rode off to save the day
A sudden tug to Tom's sleeve, you're not going to believe
Hash, ravioli, and spam, even cream corn in the can

Rolled to a stop, grabbed some groovy cans
Raced back as fast as we could
Rolled to a stop, slammed on the brakes
Looking as cool as we should

Bikes parked at their sides, tinkering to tune their rides
Being different is how we win, hope the judges appreciate the spin
Hair tangled in a mess, looking like a rat's nest
Hurry up and do your best, no room to second guess

Stick to the plan, ease onto the end
Smiling don't wear a frown
Stick to the plan, keep it rock-n-rolling
No one's going to take away my crown

All Sally do is brag, second place ain't half bad
Sally can't buy a win this time, call the police report a crime
All rise for this year's judges, hope Mr. B won't hold any grudges
Safety is the priority, the judges said with authority

Stick to the plan, ease onto the end
Smiling don't wear a frown
Stick to the plan, keep it rock-n-rolling
No one's going to take away my crown
Stick to the plan, ease onto the end
Smiling don't wear a frown
Stick to the plan, keep it rock-n-rolling
No one's going to take away my crown
No one's going to take away my crown

Chapter 8

An Idea

"Not a moment to spare," the woman said, pinning the entry number seventy to Tom's chest. Her spindly arm flailed in circles, rushing him through the gate. The rusty hinges creaked as the gate closed and bumped the Sting Ray's rear mag tire, nudging Tom onto the field.

Tom jogged to Mike and Frank without looking back. "I thought you guys bailed on me back at the barber shop."

"No way, man," Mike said. "We were running out of time." Mike pushed ahead and took the lead in the direction of the other contestants.

"We would've been eliminated from the contest without those three cans of food," Frank said as he broke into a jog and pushed the Blue Lightning beside Mike.

"We gave our word to Mr. B," Mike said as he picked up the pace. "We couldn't let our neighbors down."

Frank said. "We knew we would have to work together to make the contest in time." Frank inhaled a quick breath and sped up before continuing. "We decided to race to Mike's house and raid his mom's pantry."

"We lucked out," Mike said.

"Yeah! We were halfway there when we stopped on the corner of Oak and Elm to catch our breath." Frank lengthened his stride. "We were leaning against a bright orange, metal trash can."

Mike abruptly stopped. He waited for Tom to roll up, tugged on his T-shirt sleeve, and said, "This is the part you're not going to believe."

"The trash can was filled to the top with cans of hash, ravioli, spam, spaghetti, tuna fish, chicken soup, and all kinds of canned vegetables," Frank said, braking to a stop.

Mike yanked Tom's sleeve several times more while saying, "We grabbed three cans from the top of the pile and raced back to the park."

"Hoo-ha!" Frank shouted.

"You were busy in the closet looking for the toolbox," Mike said as the three began to roll toward the stage. "We couldn't wait any longer."

Frank sniffed his hands and sneezed. "My hands still stink from that blue goo." He brushed some stink on the back of Mike's shirt and snickered. "It was the only chance we had."

"That was wicked smart," Tom said. "You guys saved the day for me."

"Yeah, you're right," Mike said.

"Yeah, and we didn't have to read it from a book," Frank said.

The boys laughed, stopped, and took the time to slap high fives.

The three friends strolled up to the competition. Each contestant was paired side-by-side with their bicycle, evenly spaced in rows of ten.

"This has to be the largest number of people competing ever," Mike said.

"Look at all those different bikes," Frank said. "I hope we have a chance to win."

The boys wandered to the first row, looking for a place to park their bikes. A few competitors tinkered to complete last-minute tune-ups. Others posed with their bikes as their families snapped Polaroids.

"See that red and white bicycle, the one with a lot of rust on the frame?" Tom asked as he pointed to the left.

"I see it." Mike said.

"I saw one just like that in Buck's garage. That's an original 1930s Colson Flyer," Tom said. He pointed over the first two rows. "Over there, at the end of the third row is a 1955 Norman."

Mike looked side-to-side over the competitors. "Norman. You mean like the motorcycle company?"

The boys' pace slowed as they continued through the maze of bicycles.

"Yeah." Tom stretched his neck upward and pointed three rows to the left. "Those three bikes in the fifth row are a Schwinn Starlet, a Schwinn Panther, and a Schwinn Hornet."

Mike slowed to a crawl and fell behind Tom and Frank. "How are we going to compete against bikes made by these big companies?" he asked.

The boys' excitement dwindled with each step, and they slumped over their handlebars from the weight of the competition.

"Yeah, we're just three kids putting pieces of old bikes together in our garages," Frank said. "We don't stand a chance."

Tom came to a sudden stop. "Buck's garage is like a museum for bikes. He's an expert on bicycles, and he told me that our bikes are original."

Tom's eyes shined with a twinkle of excitement. "Buck never saw a bike like ours, and you don't see another bike on this field like our three." The Sting Ray rested against Tom's thin waist as he cupped his hands over Mike and Frank's shoulders. "We're different, and that's how we're going to win that prize."

"Let's hope the judges appreciate us for making something different," Mike said. "Mr. B didn't seem too impressed."

"It's Show Time"
John W. Nassivera & Bob Bates

This year's contest is now in session
Who will win, is the big question
Bike after bike stopped at center stage
Complete silence as the judges engaged

Frames, seats, handlebars, and tires
Helped us stand apart from all the others
Come closer, I'll tell you a secret
How much fun it is to be different, to be different

Lift up your head out of the sand
See me for me and clap your hands
Lift up your heart, sing with the band
Look to my soul for who I am

Boys in single file, raced up the ramp
Popped monster wheelies and rode like champs
Slammed on stage with the heavy sound of thunder
The judges raised their heads and began to wonder

Bikes screeching, a 90-degree slide
All three skidded to a rest, side-by-side.
From three blocks away it was clear
Half the town screamed the loudest cheered, the loudest cheer

Thank you for all your participation
Let's continue to enjoy the celebration
The parade will stop in the center of town
This year's winner will be crowned

Lift up your head out of the sand
See me for me and clap your hands
Lift up your heart and sing with the band
Look to my soul for who I am

Quiet Morning in The Village by Kendall McKernon

Chapter 9

It's Show Time

"People get frightened of things they don't understand," Tom said.

"Maybe Mr. B was afraid of being crushed by a charging bike," Mike said.

Frank jumped up and pointed to the back row. "There's only seven bikes in that row. Let's grab the last three places." He took off, running.

Tom zig-zagged between contestants and their bikes. Mike made chase right behind him. Within five seconds, all three boys flipped their kickstands downward and laid claim to their spot in row seven.

"Hey. Is that Sally in front of our row?" Tom pointed to the stage.

Frank stood on his toes. "That's her," he said. "Wherever Sally is, Bobby can't be too far away."

Mike scanned the contestants in his search for Bobby and said, "That kid is always trashing people." He clenched his right hand into a fist and smacked it into his left palm. "I can't wait to get my hands on that kid."

A tall, slender man towered like a beanpole over the podium and called out, "All rise for this year's judges."

Three judges dressed in black, long, flowing robes walked onto the stage and stood behind a table in front of three chairs.

"Judges Mrs. Fisher, Mr. Irish, and Mr. B presiding," the man said.

Mr. B grasped the handle of a wooden gavel and struck the tabletop three times. "This contest is now in session," Mr. B's voice rang out over the crowd of contestants. "Will the clerk please swear in the contestants?"

The man behind the podium raised his right hand slightly above his right shoulder and requested, "Will all contestants remain standing and raise your right hand?" All seventy contestants stood next to their bikes and raised their right hands.

"Do each of you swear that you are here today to come together as one community, so help you God?"

"I do!" roared through the park. The contestants followed up with, "So, help me God."

Mr. B struck the gavel twice to the table and proclaimed, "Let the contest begin."

The first contestant wheeled her bike onto the stage and stopped, front and center. The judges sat side-by-side behind the table, pointed to the handlebars, and wrote on clipboards.

The boys watched as bike after bike went across the stage. The judges honked horns, kicked tires, yanked on chains, and even sat on seats. Mr. Irish flipped one bike upside-down and inspected the entire frame with a magnifying glass.

Finally, after fifty-three minutes, the seventh row was next. Tom bent over the chrome headlight on his bike. He studied the reflection of his blurry, oval-shaped face, parted his hair down the middle of his head, and stroked his bangs behind each ear.

"What are you doing?" Frank asked with a puzzled look.

Tom pulled them into a huddle and whispered, "If we're gonna have a chance to win, we need Mr. B to think that I got my haircut. We want him to focus on our bikes and not my shag." Tom spit into his palms and flattened his bangs to the side of his head. "Hopefully, this new hair style will trick him into thinking I got my haircut." He took a quick peek over the two boys at the stage.

"I hope it works," Mike snickered, trying not to smile.

"What's so funny?" snapped Tom.

Mike broke into an uncontrollable laugh, which triggered Frank into giggles.

"Mr. B is definitely going to notice your hair." Frank said, chuckling.

Tom stroked his hands across his skull, massaging his slicked down hair over and under. The brown locks twisted and tangled into a matted mess.

"You look like you have a rat's nest on your head," Mike said, shaking his head disapprovingly.

Tom dropped his chin to his chest and vigorously whirled and twirled his head. He stopped, swept his fingers through the topsy-turvy mess, tossed his head back, and gently fluffed his hair up like a pillow. Tom dropped his hands, and his bangs fell back in place.

Mike and Frank shook their heads in approval.

"All right, every bike here is a different size or color," Tom said. "It's our frames, seats, handlebars, and tires that help us stand apart from the others."

"You're right," Frank said. "Our bikes are different, but will that be enough?"

Tom stood between Mike and Frank with his arms wrapped over their shoulders. "I have a plan." He squeezed their heads together. "Bring it in close."

The boys chewed over their assignments and tightly huddled to conceal their secret plan. After a couple of minutes, they shook their heads up and down in agreement and broke from the pack.

"It's got to work," Tom said. "Now, let's go show everyone here how much fun it is to be different."

The seventh row slowly moved one bike at a time closer to the stage. Tom, Mike, and Frank were the last in line, patiently waiting.

Sally Smite strolled onto the stage. The thin, metal spokes sparkled inside the chrome rims as the whitewall tires spun beneath a sleek, glossy, lemon-yellow frame. She wore white skips, sky-blue capris pants, and a lemon-yellow blouse. A sky-blue bow with lemon-yellow polka dots tied her blonde hair back into a ponytail. She pranced to a stop at the judges' table.

"What kind of bike is that?" Frank whispered.

"I've never seen one like it, but something looks familiar," Tom said.

"I bet her father bought it for her," Mike said. "She always gets what she wants. Her dad is super rich."

"Shush. I want to hear what the judges are saying," Tom said.

"Hello, Sally," Mr. B said. "How's your dad?"

Sally bowed and curtsied to the judges. "He's just fine, sir," she said with a bright smile. "He asked that I request your presence for dinner this Sunday."

Mike leaned into his friends and whispered, "There she goes, kissing up."

"Tell your dad it would be my pleasure," Mr. B said, smiling. "I would never pass up the chance to eat a delicious meal prepared by your mother. So, let's take a look at your bike."

"See?" Mike nudged Tom in the ribs. "I told you so."

Mr. Irish bent down on one knee and read a tin badge on the yellow frame, "Schwinn Roadster." He reached to the front tire and squeezed the spokes between his thumb and index finger. Scribbling something onto his clipboard, he called out, "This bike is a racer. Its frame is made of a new aluminum alloy that makes it lighter than any other bicycle."

Mr. B said, "That's different from any bike we've seen today."

Frank slapped his hand to his knee and whimpered, "Being different was how we were going to win. Now what?"

"Just stick to our plan," Tom said.

Mr. B wrote on his clipboard and smiled at Sally.

"My dad won a bike contest when he was my age," Sally said, smiling back.

Mr. B stopped writing and dropped his pen to the clipboard. "You're right, Sally. I remember that contest very well. I competed against your dad in that one."

Sally looked down to the stage for a moment and then back into Mr. B's face, still smiling. She politely said, "My dad told me your bike was top-notch and it was a fierce competition." Sally softly laid her hand on Mr. B's elbow and said, "Second place isn't half bad."

"You're right, Sally. Second place is something to be proud of." Mr. B dropped his clipboard onto the judges' table. "I still have the ribbon that I was awarded. It sits on my bookshelf right next to my second-place spelling bee trophy." He rubbed his chin in thought. "If I remember correctly, your father won first place in that contest, too."

Sally started to walk her bike forward. "I want to be just like my dad."

Mr. B lifted his pen and the clipboard from the table with a smile. "You're wonderful as you are."

Sally curtsied, saying, "See you at dinner tomorrow." She pranced to the end of the stage and walked down the ramp.

Mike turned to Tom and asked, "How were you ever friends with her?"

"She's nice," Tom said.

Frank said, "Sally has been angry at us the whole summer. It's gotten worst since she started hanging out with Bobby."

Tom dropped his head as the boys inched closer to the stage. "Alright, we're up," he said.

The three boys pealed out, spraying grass above their heads into the crowd of bike fans. They raced in single file up the ramp, popped wheelies, and rode across the stage with their long front forks lifted above the judges' table. Then, the three, odd, small front tires slammed to the stage with the sound of thunder. Brakes screeched, and all three bikes skidded into a 90-degree slide and came to rest, side-by-side. The boys faced out toward the crowd and sixty-seven contestants. There was a moment of silence as the judges jumped to their feet behind the table.

Tom, Mike, and Frank jumped off their banana seats and waved over their ape hanger handlebars to the crowd. The contestants and crowd went nuts. They clapped and cheered so loud that paradegoers three blocks away looked up the street.

Whack! Whack! Whack! The gavel slammed to the table.

Mr. B pushed the table to the side and pounced next to Tom at the front of the stage.

Tom dropped his head, and the palms of his hands began to sweat.

Mr. B stepped forward, glaring straight through Tom, and announced to the crowd, "Now, that was an entrance."

The audience burst into cheers. Tom looked to Mike and Frank, who shrugged. The three boys paused before stepping to the front of the stage and taking their curtain call.

"We got this contest in the bag," Tom said to his friends.

"Sally can't buy a win this time," Mike said.

The applause calmed to silence, and the contestants looked to the judges for their verdict.

Mr. B yelled out, "We now ask that all contestants remain in line and move to the Fire House. We will then begin the parade."

The contestants gazed across the stage, and a buzz grew to the chatter of who won.

Mr. B raised his voice over the jawing and said, "The parade will stop at Juckett Park in the center of town, where the winners of the bicycle contest will be announced by this year's Grand Marshall." The tittle-tattle hushed, and the contestants readied their bicycles. "Thank you all for your participation," Mr. B said. "Let's continue to enjoy this celebration as one community."

The contestants gathered their bikes and slowly rambled out into the field. The once organized straight lines became sixty-seven contestants aimlessly roaming amongst hundreds of fans like cattle on the open range.

Tom waved his friends forward and started to roll the Sting Ray to the exit ramp.

"Hold on boys," Mr. B said, holding his hand up. "You're not done yet."

Mr. Irish walked to the back of Tom's bike and bent down on one knee. Tom watched as Mr. Irish jerked the bicycle chain upward.

"There's no play between the chain and gear. It's a clean tight fit," Mr. Irish said, joggling the tire inches above the stage. "Perfect," he said.

Mr. B took a step closer and gave Tom a grim look. "I see that you fixed your chain, but it looks like you forgot to get that haircut."

The heat of the boys' excitement was cooled by Mr. B's stern face.

"Mr. Irish, take a close look for any design problems," instructed Mr. B. "Safety is the first priority."

Mr. Irish pulled his magnifying glass from a black leather bag resting under the judges' table. He squatted on the back of his heels and began to inspect each link of the Sting Ray's chain.

Mr. B jotted something down in his notes. "These three bikes were built by these boys in their garages with old, used parts." He clicked his pen open, closed it, and opened it again before continuing to scribble on his clipboard. "We don't want them riding off into the future and running over some innocent bystander."

Mike stood with his hands folded in prayer. "We went into the barber shop," he said.

Mr. Irish pulled a tape measure and protractor from the pocket protector inside the breast pocket. He took several measurements of the small front tire and angles of the extended forks from the Renegade. He sat at the table, performed multiple calculations with a slide rule, and recorded the data on his clipboard.

"Yeah, Buck helped me fix my bike," Tom said. "We ran out of time for a haircut."

Frank watched Mr. Irish get up from the table, walk over to the Blue Lightning, and measure the connection angle between the ape hanger handlebars and the frame. He became fearfully worried and said, "Mike and I raced to get three cans of creamed corn so we could all help our neighbors in need."

"Without Buck, Mike, and Frank's help, I wouldn't have been able to enter my bike into the contest," Tom said.

Mr. Irish measured the height of the Renegade's sissy bar, scribbled something onto the paper, erased it, and scribbled again. "I have all the information I need," he said to Mr. B.

Chapter 10

The Challenge

The boys walked their bikes down from the stage into the heavy traffic of volunteers marching and scampering through the field like a colony of ants collectively working to transform the park into a carnival.

Frank scuffed his toe on a half-buried stone and groaned, "Ouch!" He hopped to the Dog Stand, removed his sneaker, and rubbed his big toe.

Mr. Cutler clobbered his last nail into the hotdog stand and tucked the claw hammer through the loop of a worn-out leather toolbelt hanging from his hips. The brownish orange dogs simmered in the pot, bobbing and tumbling through the boiling current. The carpenter picked up the stainless-steel prongs and plucked a frank from the bubbling hot water. Tucking the dog into a partially sliced bun, he said, "Those bikes sure look crazy." He garnished the wiener with four squirts of mustard, one splash of ketchup, and a smear of relish while asking, "Are they safe to ride?"

"They're the safest bikes on the planet," Mike said, glaring into the booth.

Mr. Cutler chomped down on the carnival cuisine, swallowing half the dog without a single chew. He wiped a glob of red-yellowish green slobber from his chin into a white napkin and said, "I've never seen a bike like that." He took a second bite of the dog, his teeth just missing the edge of his fingertips. "They sure are different. Are you sure those bicycles are safe?"

"Safer than that frankfurter you just choked down," Mike said.

"I read that hotdogs are made of pink slime, and meat slurry." Tom pointed to the pot and asked, "Are they cooked all the way through?"

"You don't want to get botulism," Frank said. "I hear bacteria grows in hotdogs, if they aren't cooked for at least an hour."

"One time, I got food poisoning and had diarrhea for two days," Tom said.

Mr. Cutler gagged and retched.

Frank heaved at the sight of Mr. Cutler swallowing his last bite a second time.

Mike turned to Tom with a giggle and smirked. "Good one."

"Common, let's get to the fire barn," Tom said.

The engines slowly rolled out of the Fire House. Firemen dressed in black rubber boots, brown turnout jackets, and bright yellow helmets swarmed around the monstrous, red trucks. Doors swung open and slammed closed as firemen scrambled into positions behind the steering wheel, in the cab, and on top of the running boards and rear chrome bumpers. The ladder truck pulled ahead, followed by a pumper, and then EMS. The three trucks slowly crawled around the corner onto Main Street and stopped. Twenty-four men and women volunteers wearing their dress blues, white bell caps, and black leather shoes scurried to line up in a single row on both sides of the trucks.

Tom flipped the kickstand down, mounted the banana seat, leaned back against the sissy bar, and said, "It looks like we're going to have a long wait."

Frank leaned out between the ape hangers over the teardrop headlight. "Check it out," he said. "There's Billy and Joseph in their Boy Scout uniforms."

Mike pushed up from his seat and stood on the pedals, wavering over the frame for a split second before catching his balance. He cupped his hands to his brow and scanned the crowded block. "Where? I don't see them."

"Right behind the EMS, holding the banner for Troop Fifty-Four." Frank leaned further through the handlebars and pointed at the fire trucks. "They look like army soldiers in those uniforms."

"Those uniforms are cool," Mike said. "I tried to join the Boy Scouts once."

"What happened?" Frank asked.

Mike tucked his chin to his chest and said, "I couldn't start a fire."

Frank said, "I'm good at that. Maybe I'll join."

"I wonder who the Grand Marshal is this year?" Tom yawned, sitting with his eyes closed. His skinny, long arms were folded across his chest with his fingers tucked tightly in his armpits. Tom's knobby knees were locked between the chrome handlebars, and he stretched his bony legs straight out over the extended lime green forks.

"Usually it's a politician, like the mayor, or a war veteran, like Buck's son," Mike said as he fell back onto his seat. "Someone who has made a sacrifice to make this a better place."

"It's not Mayor Muff." Frank pointed to his left at a large, brick building expanding over a half a block. The Masonic Temple stood five stories high, making it the largest building in town. "See all those classic cars lining up behind the 4-H group? He's sitting in the rumble seat of that antique Model Ford."

"What does 4-H stand for?" Mike asked.

Tom pinched his shoulder blades together, reclined into the sissy bar, stretched both arms over his head, and groaned, "Head, heart, hands, and health."

"So, it's a club for kids who want to become doctors?" Mike asked.

Tom moaned as he sat up straight and cleared his throat. "Not really. The 4-H organization helps young people become good neighbors." Tom cleared his throat a second time. "You know, like when Mr. B asked us to bring a can of food to help people in need."

The boys' chat was interrupted by a black and white police cruiser's flashing red lights from its party hat. The car slowed to a stop several yards to the left of the boys. A uniformed officer exited the driver's side and walked to the front of the car. He blew a tin whistle and began to direct the groups into position for the parade.

Thrilled and excited, Frank turned to Tom and said, "This is gonna be so cool."

Tom flopped forward over the banana seat, clumsily fumbling with the gear shifter. He grunted as the gear shifter clicked into second, clacked back into first, clicked twice into third, and then clacked back into first.

"I hope one of us wins this contest," Tom groaned. "We worked so hard. One of us deserves to win first prize."

Mike inched his bike toward the policeman directing contestants.

Frank asked, "What would you do with fifty dollars, anyways?"

"I told you. I'm going to buy a brand-new Project J-38 Spyder. I've been dreaming about riding it to school for months."

"Why would you waste money on a new bike?" Mike stopped inching forward, stood tall over the banana seat, and pointed down. "Look at what we have."

"Our bikes are different from anyone else's in the contest, and we built them together," Frank said. "That's better than any new bike."

"You wish," said a snotty voice from over Frank's left shoulder. Sally Smite sauntered up to the boys, swirling her ponytail into a bun and twiddling the sky-blue bow with lemon-yellow polka dots into a knot. She stopped in the middle of the boys, folded her arms across her chest, and sassed, "Oh, your bikes are different, alright."

"That's right," Mike snapped as he held out both hands. "Made by our hands, just as we planned."

"Those broken-down bikes are no competition for my Roadster." Sally spoke with tightly puckered lips, "My bike is the best money can buy." She then folded her arms across her chest. "I'm going to win this contest."

Frank leaped from the Blue Lightning and stepped up to Sally. "One man's trash is another man's treasure."

"You saw the crowd go wild when we road onto the stage," snapped Tom.

"Your bike is a lemon, just like its color," Mike said, waving goodbye to Sally. "Go home and tell your dad he wasted his money."

"All you can do is pop a wheelie," Sally said, clenching her hips with both hands. She threw her shoulders back and stuck her pointed nose up to the sky. "Your bikes couldn't beat the garbage truck you pulled the parts from."

"Anytime!" Tom said, jumping from his seat and pointing straight at Sally. "You tell us when and where. I'll be there!"

Sally turned her back, took three steps, and stopped. She slowly turned to Tom and said, "Will you show up this time?"

Tom slumped and stuttered, "Ya, you don't under…stand. I didn't have any…"

"How about right now?" Sally pointed to the corner of the Fire Station. "Right there."

"Ready Set Go"
John W. Nassivera & Bob Bates

What a strange sight, nothing looks quite right
Made by your hands, now that's a silly plan
Believe your eyes, best money can buy
That's right baby, there's no maybe

Now let's race, don't come in last place
Stop your silly stories, without guts there's no glory
First to grab a brass medallion, off a wooden stallion
Tag the silver flagpole, finish wins gold

Ready Set and Go, take this deadly blow
Left you for defeat, piled in a heap
Tools scattering, teeth chattering
Left you way below, three behind, the lead is mine
Ready Set Go...

Zig zag with a thrill, horses quietly still
Slapping browbands, with both my hands
Spotted a brass idol, mount on a leather bridle
I see your back, it's time for a new attack

Horses slowly prance, you don't stand a chance
That black Thoroughbred, bucken and fled
Hooves smartly clomping with thunderous stomping
I just found a stack, I'm first to race back

Ready Set and Go, and take this deadly blow
Left you for defeat, piled up in a heap
Tools scattering, teeth chattering
Left you way below, three behind, the lead is mine
Ready Set Go...

Chapter 11

Get Out of The Way

Bobby Holler stood to the left of the fire station. Standing five feet, two inches tall and weighing one hundred and twelve pounds, Bobby was a behemoth of a fifth grader, dwarfing Tom, Mike, and Frank.

Mike and Frank flipped their kickstands up and barreled past Sally to the station house. Mike skidded to a stop at Bobby's feet.

"Who are you looking at?" Mike snarled, glaring straight into Bobby's eyes.

Bobby bent forward, inches from Mike's face, and breathed like a raging bull. A low, guttural growl raged upward within his throat, "I'm looking at you…"

The Blue Lightning bumped over Bobby's left foot and braked onto his right.

"Ouch!" wailed Bobby. His body recoiled as his shoulders cringed, and he yelled with a grimace, "Get off my foot!"

Frank said, "Oh, sorry." He backed off Bobby's right foot and rolled up onto his left.

"Ow!" yelped Bobby. "Doggone, gosh-darn, cripes. Get off!"

"Oh. Sorry." Frank giggled and rolled off.

Bobby hopped and limped to the side of the Fire Station, whimpering like a hurt puppy.

"What a big baby." Mike said, puckering his lips and puffed his cheeks. "Baby Bobby got a booboo."

Tom rolled to a stop and said, "You ready to race fair, or do you and Bobby still want to play games?"

"My Roadster is the fastest bike on the planet," Sally said. "I can beat your piece of junk with my eyes closed."

"Keep your eyes open," Tom said, shifting the Sting Ray into first gear. "You may want to take a snapshot of my rear fender when I cross the finish line in front of you."

Sally pointed out across the field to Margret Murphy Elementary School. Paris Park was teeming with neighbors erecting food stands, carnival rides, and gaming booths, as well as stoking the hot coals of twenty barbeques for tonight's chicken roast.

"First person to race to the school, touch the flagpole, and get back wins," Tom said.

"What kind of sissy challenge is that?" smirked Sally. "The first one to zoom past the Shoot-the-Chutes, zip between the Teacups and Magic Sombrero rides, grab a ring from a wooden horse on the Merry-Go-Round, tag the flagpole, and get back to the fire station wins."

Tom surveyed the field of one-hundred or more men, women, and children scurrying through the race path. The long, extended front forks of a wheelie bike would make it very difficult to control through the tight turns and narrow paths at high speeds.

Bobby leaned into the back of Sally's ear and whispered, "Good call."

"My spying paid off," Sally whispered.

"There's too many people," Tom said. "Let's stay away from the rides and keep the race safe."

"No guts, no glory," Sally said. "What are you, a scaredy-cat?"

Mike stood above his bike, grimaced at Sally, and shouted, "It's on! Stop flapping your jaw and start the race."

Bobby hobbled several yards from the corner of the Fire House. He kicked his heel into the dirt, dragging it like a garden hoe for ten feet, and etched a starting line into the ground.

Frank rolled up to the line, followed by Mike. Tom's wheelie tire thumped over the shallow rut and skidded to a stop. He dropped his feet to the ground and shuffled heel-to-toe back behind the line.

A pair of yellow, pastel-colored racing gloves dangled from Sally's waist, tucked tightly beneath a blue belt. She slowly sauntered to the side of the Roadster and jostled the gloves over each individual finger. Bobby held the bike balanced while Sally mounted and slipped her feet into a pair of silver toe-clips. "Stick to the plan," Sally muttered to Bobby.

Tom stared straight ahead, squeezed down on the gear lever, and said to himself, "This is my time to show them who's cool."

Bobby walked out in front of the racers with a black and white checkered flag neatly rolled and tucked under his left armpit. He stopped and faced the four competitors. "Where did you find that piece of junk?" Bobby said to Tom. "You were better off not having a bike." He reached beneath his armpit and slowly drew the flag like a sabre from its sheathing.

"Racers ready," Bobby commanded. Whipping the flag open, he raised both arms above his head and said, "Racers, hold your positions."

Sally jumped the start, thwacking the front forks of the Sting Ray with a hammer kick.

"Go!" Bobby jumped into the air while swirling the flag above his head, twirling it out to his side, and thrusting it down to the ground.

Tom's wheelie tire careened into the Renegade, leaving the two bikes in a tangled mess at the starting line. The Blue Lightning bolted past the crash straight at Bobby, who stood as a human roadblock, barricading Sally from her competitors.

"I dare you to try and get by." Bobby waved Frank forward.

Frank stopped and slid off the front of the banana seat to his feet. He chomped his bottom lip, squinted his eyes, and shook his head, accepting the challenge. The Blue Lightning surged forward.

"Get out of the way!" Frank shouted.

Bobby lunged forward, wildly whipped the flag side-to-side, and thrashed at his challenger. The flag cut through the air inches above Frank's head and clobbered the sissy bar, splintering it in half. The impact sent shivers through Bobby's body.

"He...Hey, you...u bbbbroke my flaaag!" he stammered.

"Get out of the way, you big baboon," Mike hollered from behind.

The Renegade's front tire rose from the ground as if it was going to swallow Bobby whole. Mike charged full speed ahead.

Bobby dropped, tumbled, and rolled. He sat on the ground with his face red with sweat and dirt smudged across his cheeks. "You'll pay for that!" Bobby shook a closed fist at Mike.

The Sting Ray stormed by, spewing a cloud of dust into the air. Tom shifted into third gear, zoomed pass the Shoot-the-Chutes, and pulled beside Mike. The two caught sight of Frank.

Frank closed the gap on Sally, snugging tightly behind the Roadster's rear wheel as they pedaled between the Teacups and Magic Sombrero. Volunteers worked diligently, hammering, drilling, and bolting the rides together. Two workers scrambled between the rides, lugging a heavy steel beam while others scampered back and forth, carrying tools. Frank made his move to pass Sally. He stood on the pedals, thrusting and pumping with all his might. The Blue Lightning bolted forward, pulled beside the Roadster, and flashed into the lead by a tire length.

Sally countered by steering into the path of several volunteers, forcing them to leap out of her way. A bald man with a goatee fell to the ground in front of Frank. Hammers, screwdrivers, wrenches, nuts, and bolts spilled from his toolbox as it tumbled, flipped, and crashed to the ground.

Frank clasped the handbrakes tightly, turning his knuckles white. The Blue Lightning shuttered out of control, rattling all thirty-two teeth in Frank's head. His fingers cramped and throbbed. The bike skidded to a stop, less than an inch from the fallen volunteer's chin.

Pinned to the ground, the man looked up between the tarnished spokes and gulped a sigh of relief.

"Let me help you up, sir." Frank rolled off the man's beard and extended his hand downward.

"That was some crackerjack driving," said the volunteer, patting the dirt from his pants. Sweat rolled over his glistening cheeks as his fingers combed the dirt from his straggly pointed beard. "Lucky for me, you rode that bike like an ace."

Frank got down on his hands and knees and helped to gather every nut, bolt, and tool. "Thanks, sir."

Tom whizzed by with the Renegade on his side and shouted back at Frank, "We got this!"

Sally raced up to the Merry-Go-Round and braked to a stop. The wooden horses stood quietly still as the carousel sat motionless. She jumped from her seat and zigged back and forth, mounting and dismounting the brightly painted horses in search for a single brass ring.

Tom and Mike skidded to a stop.

"Look, over there," Mike said. "On the Appaloosa horse, with the white patch splotched on its rear. It's Sally!"

"We've lucked out." Tom sprung from the banana seat. "She hasn't found a ring yet."

The boys leaped onto the circular platform and ran in the opposite direction from Sally.

Tom said, "I'll check the horses on the outside, and you search the horses lining the inside."

The boys searched high and low, slapping browbands and thumping saddle horns. The distance between the two boys and Sally closed as the competitors frantically searched.

"Over there. Six horses in front of us, on your side." Mike pointed over the saddle of a white Arabian stallion. "There's a brass ring mounted on the bridle of that black Thoroughbred with the white star on its forehead."

Tom looked across the Merry-Go-Round for Sally. A huge, wooden post in the center of the circular platform blocked his view. Sally emerged from behind the control panel mounted halfway up the post. He scurried forward between the wooden horses and darted for the Thoroughbred.

To the right of the panel, the word "On" was painted beside an arrow pointing to the floor. Sally thrusted the starter clutch down. The ten-ton platform jerked forward, throwing Tom to the floor planks beneath the stomping hooves.

Sally leaned forward and pinched her fingers against an iron rod as the clutch plunged downward. Twelve brass rings laid stacked at the end of the rod. The white star Thoroughbred broke into a wild gallop. Mike charged forward, dashing into the fleeing herd as Sally struggled to pull her fingers free. She shimmied her hand lose, grabbed a ring, zigged through the stampede of carrousel horses, jumped from the platform, and sped off on her Roadster.

Mike leaped from the platform onto the banana seat of the Renegade with the brass ring and sped off. "Let's go."

Tom pulled himself up to his feet, jumped onto his seat, and made chase.

Mike caught up to Sally, thirty yards from the main doors to the school. The custodian walked out dressed in grey denim coveralls. A name tag reading "Ronnie" was sewed to his chest pocket.

The two jockeyed for the inside position as they approached the hairpin turn around the flagpole. Sally pushed, elbowed, and bumped Mike, but he out-muscled her and took the lead by more than a bicycle length.

Tom shifted into fifth gear and continued, full speed ahead. He was now two bicycle lengths behind Sally and closing.

Mike turned tight into the flagpole, releasing his left hand from the handlebars. He shifted his butt off the edge of the seat and leaned outward. The Renegade dipped sideways. With his arm stretched out straight, he reached to make the tag.

Out of nowhere, janitor Ronnie stepped from behind the pole, holding the flag folded in a triangular blue field with white stars.

"Yeeeow!" shouted Mike, skidding off course.

"What the heck?" Ronnie screamed. He threw his hands into the air, launching the folded flag, which spun like a helicopter propeller into the sky.

"Don't let the flag touch the ground!" Ronnie shouted.

Sally leaned tight into the flagpole, with Tom looping outside to avoid any contact with the custodian. He squeezed both handbrakes, screeching to a stop.

"Coming through! Get out of my way!" Sally screeched. Her yellow glove was outstretched to make the tag.

The janitor ducked in the nick of time as Sally's hand slapped the pole inches above his head.

Tom's gangly arms reached out over the ten-inch wheelie tire and made a fingertip catch. "Got it!" he shouted.

Mike flung the brass ring into the air and waved his hands. "Toss the flag to me."

With the brass ring clenched in his hand, Tom sped off after Sally.

"Go, go, go!" shouted Mike. "You can still beat her to the fire barn."

Sally was one-hundred yards from the barn. Tom would have to expend every last ounce of his energy to catch her. He shifted directly into fifth gear and stood up on his pedals, pumping every stroke with all of his might. He was making up ground, but Sally was now fifty yards from the finish line.

A dozen volunteers rolled twelve hand trucks stacked six cases high with soda pop. The wall of pop marched in single file twenty feet short of the finish line. Sally was forced to stop.

Tom raced forward, closing the distance between him and Sally by thirty yards, then twenty yards, then ten yards, and then ten feet. Sally took off, forcing the last three volunteers to stop in their tracks, and opened a hole in the line.

The two raced through the volunteers, side-by-side, only to come face-to-face with the outstretched arms of the law. They skidded to a stop at the feet of the police officer, ten feet short of the finish line. The officer towered over the two, standing rigid as a stone wall, unyielding to passage. This race was over.

"Do you know how dangerous your behavior is?" the officer sternly asked.

Sally and Tom dropped their heads in silence.

A crowd of twenty people gathered around them. The whispers of, "What just happen? Can you believe what those two kids just did?" buzzed from the group. "Kids have no respect these days."

Tom needed to say something in his defense, and he needed to say it before Sally. "I'm sorry. I…"

A shout of, "Officer, officer," echoed from behind the policeman. Things were about to get even worse for Tom. "Thief! Thief!" the voice called out from the crowd.

Bobby ran up from behind the policeman and clung to his outstretched arm. "That's the boy, officer," Bobby said, pointing at Tom. "He's the one. That bully stole my brass ring from the carousel." Bobby ran over to Tom, saying, "It's in his hand." He grasped Tom's wrist and waved his closed fist at the officer's face. "Make him open his hand."

"Open your hand, son," the policeman commanded, folding his arms across his chest. "Nice and slow."

The crowd was getting larger and had grown to more than fifty people.

"Officer, I'm no bully," Tom said, staring into the policeman's sunglasses at his own reflection.

The policeman slowly pulled his sunglasses from his face and tucked them into the front pocket of his neatly pressed button-up shirt. He sternly said, "Open your hand, son."

Tom slowly opened his hand, and the brass ring glittered in the sun.

"Thief, thief," said Bobby. "Arrest him, put him in jail."

The crowd gasped with all eyes staring directly at Tom.

Chain Links

"Stopped Red Handed"
John W. Nassivera & Bob Bates

Well... The Renegade rose from the tangled mess
Sweat and dirt smudged across Mike's chest
Blue Lightning flashed to a big lead
As Sting Ray battled to be free
The team of horses quietly watch
Tom and Mike skidded to a stop

Well... The boys had worked so hard at winning
As that floor was dizzily spinning
On a horse past an Arabian stallion
hung a single metallic medallion
Tom darted after the thoroughbred
As the carrousel stampede raced ahead

Well... Stopped by the outstretched arm of the law
By a man standing firm like a stone wall
He stood there stranded and abandoned
Accused of being caught red-handed
Tom's forehead wrinkled and creased
As he growled real loud with his gritting teeth

With the brass ring clenched in his hand
A voice yelled grab him, he's your man
Open that hand son, Nice and slow
Tom stood face-to-face with his foe
The crowd began to grow and grow
I'm innocent I tell you, don't you know

All right folks, the show is done
Back to work cause you had your fun
Nothing to see here not your concern
Stay here son when will you learn
It's safety before your fun and games
Now line up the cops and release Tom's reins

91

The Light Ahead by Kendall McKernon

Chapter 12

Something to Smile About

"I'm innocent." Tom looked into the police officer's face and pleaded, "I didn't steal this ring. You've got to believe me."

"Son, it looks to me that you've been caught red-handed." The policeman reached to his belt and rested his hand on a pair of handcuffs.

Tom's brow grew heavy, and his forehead creased as he turned to Bobby with an intense gaze. "You," snarled Tom. His nose flared as he pointed his index finger into Bobby's face. "Tell him the truth, you liar." Tom growled with bared teeth.

Mike and Frank pushed through the crowd of over one hundred spectators. "It's Bobby talking trash again," Mike said to Frank.

Bobby jumped behind the policeman and cringed. "He's crazy." Bobby peeked around the officer's hulking body. His eyes shifted to Sally, then to Tom, and back to Sally. Bobby dropped his hand to his thigh and quietly waved Sally past the officer.

All eyes were on Tom as Sally crept through the crowd with the yellow Roadster and tiptoed across the finish line unnoticed. She turned to Tom and performed a victory bow. Her head lifted, and she waved goodbye. Sally mouthed, "Who's left standing alone now?"

The corners of Tom's lip turned downward. His mind flashed back to everything that had happened so far that day, but now, he was going to be arrested. He was about to be locked out of any chance of winning the fifty dollars.

"Let me see that ring," Bobby said. He reached from behind the policeman, yanked it from Tom's hand, and held the ring an inch from his eyes. "After closer examination, this is not my brass ring," Bobby said to the policeman.

The officer blew a shriek from his whistle and ordered, "All right people, the show is over. Back to work. We have a lot to accomplish in very little time."

Frank pointed at Bobby and said to Mike, "Look at that rat scurry off."

93

"You should know not to race through a crowd of people," the policeman said. "Always put others' safety before your own fun and games." He waved his thumb over his shoulder toward the start of the parade. "Go line up before I change my mind and lock you up for disturbing the peace."

"Thank you, sir," Tom said to the officer. Frank and Mike rolled up beside Tom as the police officer went back to directing the bicycle contestants into the proper marching position.

"Hey, Tom. Are you okay?" Mike asked. He patted Tom on the back. "Sally would do anything to win."

"First, that punk Bobby and his friends made fun of me at school." Tom wrenched his closed fists around the handlebars. "Now, he made me look foolish in front of one hundred people. I can't wait to win this contest and buy that new bike."

"We got your back," Frank said. He looked out over the contestants lining up. "Sally and Bobby will get what's coming to them."

The policeman blew his whistle and pointed for Mike to pull up in front of him, four feet from the street curb. The officer took several steps to his left and waved Tom to the middle of the street. The Sting Ray's long, lime-green front forks stretched down the center of the double yellow line. The officer maneuvered Frank into the last position. The three wheelie bikes stretched across the street to complete the parade.

The officer swaggered up to the Sting Ray. Tom slumped down into the banana seat and stared into the dark tar of the asphalt. The late afternoon sun shimmered off the polished police badge. The officer's name tag read

"Thompson." Tom wanted to hide as Officer Thompson stared down at the lime-green bike.

"That's some fancy bike, son," Officer Thompson said with respect and approval. "Enjoy the parade."

Tom bounced up straight and proud. "Thank you, sir."

The officer walked back to the cruiser and climbed into the driver's seat. Tom looked back over his shoulder and saw the policeman reach below the dashboard. He pulled a two-wave radio mic to his lips.

Seconds later, the fire trucks' roof-mounts rotated red and blue beams of light out onto the buildings and captured the parade audience's attention. The three engines' sirens wailed, signaling the start of the parade. A roar of excitement erupted and echoed south down Main Street.

Frank turned to his friends and shouted over the noise, "Let's have some fun!"

"This is it. We're going to find out who won." Tom yelled over the applause of the crowd, "Juckett Park, here we come!"

The lights on top of the fire engines whirled as the trucks rolled forward. The ear-piercing shriek of the sirens slowly silenced. Billy, Joseph, and Boy Scout Troop Fifty-Four marched forward and disappeared around the corner.

The fifty-member High School Marching Band stood still, waiting in straight rows with their chins up, chests out, shoulders back, and instruments tucked under their right arms. The drum major stood front and center, dressed in a tall, plumed hat while gold chains draped across his chest. A gold whistle perched between his lips blew out, *FWEEEEEEEEEEEEE.*

The 4-H Club was next to march into the street, followed by a truck full of clowns, Cub Scouts, Brownies, a float carrying the Dairy Queen, the drum and bugle corps, and a battalion of soldiers dressed as Roger's Rangers.

The time finally came for the lines of cyclists to slowly pedal around the corner onto Main Street. The parade slowly marched forward, stopping every twenty to thirty yards and forcing the bicyclists to drop their feet to the ground and wait.

Tom moaned and groaned, "At this rate, it'll be midnight when we reach Juckett Park."

"Stop being such a parade pooper," Mike said.

The crowd lined both sides of the street, eight rows deep. Frank waved thumbs-up to his next-door neighbors, who were standing two rows back. He turned to the middle of the street. "We'll be there before you know it."

Tom's back rolled down the sissy bar as he slumped into the seat. His lips twitched, and with a sudden jerk to the handlebars, he said, "I can't take it much longer."

Mike waved to the cheering crowd. "Stop worrying. You'll miss all the fun."

The parade inched forward. A thunderous "bang" fired off a cloud of grey smoke above the parade. Everyone's attention was captured by an old pickup truck. Arms, legs, and big red clown shoes flailed, flapped, and waved out of the windows. The truck rolled to a stop next to Frank, and five clowns spilled out of the passenger's door onto the road.

"Check it out." Frank chuckled.

The clowns skipped, pranced, and frolicked to the back of the pickup. A cloud of red, white, and blue balloons floated above the truck. The clowns plucked the strings as if they were picking flowers and scampered into the crowd with bouquets of bopping and jouncing balloons.

"Over here! Over here!" Frank yelled over the laughter and cheers.

The clowns scurried and darted amongst the spectators, handing out balloons to children, parents, and grandparents alike. One clown tied a balloon to the collar of a miniature schnauzer with salt and pepper whiskers around its muzzle.

"Over here!" yelled Frank. "I'll take a balloon."

A tall, spindly clown on wooden stilts took several gawky strides between the bicyclists. Twenty to thirty balloons floated above his eight-foot-tall body. The lanky clown took three clumsy steps to the rear of the parade. He bent downward and tied three balloons, each a different color, to Frank's sissy bar.

"Check it out. This looks so cool." Frank pointed over his shoulder at the balloons. "You have to get some balloons, so we look like a team."

Tom hastily tapped his feet to the blacktop, inched his bike forward, and stomped both feet to a stop. "I don't have time for this foolishness."

At that moment, an enormous clown wearing nothing, but a jumbo-sized white cloth diaper scampered from the driver's side of the pickup onto the street. It was Diapers the Clown, and he must have weighed over three hundred pounds. His belly jiggled and joggled like jelly. He romped to the middle of the street while holding one hundred balloons over his head.

The clown frolicked through the street and danced the shimmy shake. The crowd burst out into laughter as the humongous diaper wildly shook back and forth.

"Do your thing, Diapers!" Mike waved the clown on.

The clown wobbled to the middle of the street. Diapers greeted Tom with a jolly, red smile that stretched across his round face.

One corner of Tom's mouth lifted his face into a sappy smile. He slowly slouched back against the sissy bar. He was the center of attention as the clown laughed and skipped to the back of the Sting Ray. Diapers waved both of his glove-covered hands up and down.

"Do it! Do it! Do it!" cheered the crowd.

The clown wrapped all of the strings around the chrome sissy bar, tied a bow, and took three steps back. To Tom's surprise, the mag rear wheel floated upwards. Tom wrestled with the bike to keep it on the ground. Diapers slapped his blue gloved hands to his powder-covered cheeks.

"Oh! No!" roared the crowd.

Diapers wiggled and waggled in a circle around the bike. He squeezed his cheeks, twisting his red-painted smile into a frown of alarm.

"Do something!" shouted the crowd.

Diapers grabbed the sissy bar, fell to the road, scrambled to his feet, toppled to the road, stumbled to stand, and tumbled to the road. The three hundred pounds of clown lay on his side, reached up with one hand, grabbed the sissy bar, and anchored the rear of the bike to the road. Diapers wound the strings around his wrist, then untied the knot with a twist. The balloons floated upward and tugged the whopping clown onto his two feet. The crowd roared in laughter as Diapers handed Tom a red, white, and blue balloon. He made his way across the road, jiggling and joggling from head to toe, and stopped for a brief moment to throw a smile Tom's way.

Mike tied three balloons to the back of his banana seat while laughing hysterically and yelled over to Tom, "Are you having fun yet?!"

Tom secured the red, white, and blue balloons to his sissy bar. With a smile across his face, he threw Mike a thumbs-up.

Diapers' whole body wiggled and wobbled as he romped to the driver side door of the pickup. He struggled to shimmy across the seat, jiggling and joggling his big, round belly behind the steering wheel. A knock and a pop of grey smoke rolled from under the hood. Diapers leaned his head out the window, wearing an enormous smile and beeping the horn, *Aaht aahht beeeee*ep! His hefty hand slapped the door panel as he drove away.

Tom read the flaking painted words, "Put a smile on someone's face." Smiling ear-to-ear, Tom shouted, "You're the truck driver!"

"Chance of Rainbow Showers"
John W. Nassivera, Albert Bouchard, David Hirschberg

The front line of bikes rolled through the canyon of heroes
Kids held a banner that read, We Love Our Neighbors
The boys turned their eyes back across the street
In front of the Inn patrons jumped to their feet

Armed with confetti snappers and streamers
Kaboom, paper-hovers, flutters and flickers
As the parade marched to the beat
An infantry of squirt guns kids lined the street

Orange, red, and blue
Violet, green, and yellow.
Colors across the sky
We sure look different now

Across the street, from five rows deep
A dozen fifth graders, squirmed for a peep
Front forks popped off the road
Tires whirled above their heads

On and On and On
The wheelies went On and On and On

Ten yards, then twenty, then thirty
Past Saint Paul's and on and on to Saint Mary's
The crowd showed their elation
And rowed in a standing ovation

Orange, red, and blue
Violet, green, and yellow.
Colors across the sky
We sure look different now

The three boys slammed upon their brakes

Chain Links

Tom turned a smile exploding his face
That should make them all understand
Everybody knows now who I am

Orange, red, and blue
Checkout that crazy drum set
Violet, green and yellow
And look at the size of those speakers
Colors across the sky
Hey it's almost time
Orange, red, an blue
We could be on stage standing as the leaders
Violet, green, and yellow
Give it some gas It's time to collect the cash
Colors across the sky
Things sure look different now.

The Church in Summer by Kendall McKernon

Chapter 13

Chance of Rainbow Showers

The front line of bicycles rolled through the town's canyon of heroes. Spectators cheered and shouted downward from their second and third-story apartment windows, while others applauded from fire escapes above. A large group of patrons stepped out of Nassivera's Inn and lined the street. Mike,

Tom, and Frank pedaled past the Knights of Columbus lodge and slowed to a stop in front of the Inn.

"They make the best meatballs," Tom hollered over to Mike.

"The best in the U.S." Mike said, licking his chops.

"Look!" Frank yelled, pointing to a second-floor window above the restaurant. A group of children held a paper banner that read, "We Love Our Neighbors."

Attilio, the owner and chef, stood outside the restaurant, wearing a white apron tied loosely around his waist.

"Hey Mikey," yelled Attilio. "Sei in gran forma." He pinched his index finger to his thumb and waved his hand in approval.

"What did he say?" Tom asked.

Mike turned to Tom, waved his index finger pinched to his thumb like Attilio had, and said, "We look fantastic."

"Wow! You know how to speak Italian?" Tom asked.

"Attilio taught me some words," Mike said. "He lives next door. He's my neighbor."

Attilio shouted to Mike, "Consegne per domani." He reached underneath the apron, revealing a silver chain secured to the belt loop of his trousers. Attilio pulled a round tarnished watch from his pocket, swung it from the chain, and said, "Dieci al mattino. Si?"

Mike shook his head up and down. "Yes. Tomorrow morning at ten."

"Grazie," Attilio said.

"What's going on tomorrow morning?" Tom asked.

Mike turned back to Tom and answered, "My brothers and I make deliveries for the restaurant."

"You have a job?" Tom gasped. "What else haven't you told me?"

"Sort of." Mike held his hands out to his sides. "Attilio donates lunch and dinner to the senior citizens building on Sundays, and we help him with the delivery." He shrugged. "No pay."

Attilio clasped both hands around his mouth and, like a drill sergeant, yelled out, "Attenzione!"

The boys turned their eyes back across the street, where the brigade of patrons jumped to attention in front of the Inn, armed with confetti snappers and hand-flick streamers.

Attilio counted, "Uno, due, tre."

The "kabooms" from snappers and hand-flickers blasted puffs of grey smoke and bursts of colored confetti into the sky. The rainbow of paper hovered above the cyclists' heads and then fluttered and flickered down across the street in front of the Inn, draping the three riders and their bikes in bright-colored streamers.

The parade began to march forward, and the boys pedaled camouflaged beneath a rainbow curtain of confetti. The parade quickly came to another stop. The boys dropped their feet in front of McCann's Pharmacy.

Tom peered through the streamers at Juckett Park, one-hundred feet in front of them. He flushed red with excitement and shouted, "There's the bandstand!"

Mike jumped up from his seat and thrust his arm through the confetti at the stage. "Check out that crazy drum set, and look at the size of those speakers."

The parade stretched past St. Mary's Church, turned left around the park at St. Paul's Church, and extended down the other side of the park past the First Presbyterian Church. It stopped in front of the United Methodist Church with its tall brick steeples.

"It's almost time. We could be on stage, accepting the grand prize," Tom said.

The parade advanced forward. An infantry of kids with squirt guns lined the road between the cyclists and Juckett Park. A platoon of seven boys and girls rested the barrows of their water rifles against their right shoulders.

A girl stood on the street curb, shoulder-to-shoulder with the first water gunner. Tom pointed at the platoon and called out, "It's Cyndi!"

"Where? I don't see her," Mike said as his head bobbed up and down.

Tom pointed to the crowd and shouted over the noise, "The tall girl with the curly light brown hair wearing the bright blue sun dress."

The parade came to a stop. Frank rested on Blue Lightning, three feet from Cyndi.

"Hey. What's happening?" Frank smiled as he held out his hand, palm up. "Slap me five."

Cyndi grinned with her right hand stretched straight above her wavy chestnut hair. She barked out the order, "Ready."

Frank's shoulders tensed in anticipation of a stinging slap.

The seven-water gunners raised their rifles.

105

"Aim," called out Cyndi.

Frank's face squinches as he waited for the smack.

The gunners looked up their barrows at the blue sky over the park.

Cyndi swung her arm straight down, completely missing Frank's open palm, and shouted, "Fire!"

Water sprayed like a fountain. Drops pitter-patted on their heads and trickled over the shredded ticker tape. Splotches of multi-color oozed from the paper streamers.

A second round of orders rang out, "Ready. Aim. Fire."

Water rain down, splattering and drenching the confetti. The dissolving streamers began to douse the boys.

"Ready. Aim. Fire," was ordered a third and final time. Cyndi then commanded, "Present arms. Order arms. Port arms."

The rifles dropped to the sidewalk, and the soaking stopped. The now liquid confetti washed a stream of rainbow colors over the boys' shirts, seeped into the fabric, and transformed them into a funky tie-dyed style.

Tom admired the colored splotches of red and yellow, smears of green on blue, and smudges of orange and violet across his T-shirt. "We sure look different now."

The parade moved forward as the boys joked with commander Cyndi and the seven sixth graders. Frank inspected one of the gunners' water rifle. Seeing that it was half-full, he quickly counterattacked by squirting water at Cyndi's feet. Stunned by the surprise attack, she danced into a jig to avoid getting her sneakers wet. The friends laughed hysterically, not noticing that the distance between them and the other bicyclists had grown to more than thirty yards.

"Hey, look." Mike waved to get Tom's attention. "We better get a move on," he said.

"You call those wheelie bikes?" Cyndi called out to the boys. "Let's see what you can do." The seven water gunners pointed their water rifles at the boys. "It's wheelie time."

Across the street, a dozen fifth graders had squirmed to the front of the crowd onto the curb and chanted, "Go! Go! Go!"

Tom, Mike, and Frank lined up, side-by-side, stomped down on their pedals, spun their rear tires in a fury, and burned rubber.

Streams of water shot out of the seven barrels above the crowd.

"GO!" Tom shouted.

The three popped their front forks from the road and sped straight at the park. The small front tires whirled above their heads. The bikes wheelied ten yards, then twenty yards, then thirty yards, and then past Saint Mary's Church. The boys shifted their bodies to the side of their seats, and the wheelies raced into the turn before Saint Paul's. Tom took a slight lead and dangerously released his right hand from the ape hangers. He looked out to the bandstand and waved to the crowd as they circled near First Presbyterian Church.

"Watch out!" Mike shouted in a panic.

The other sixty-seven bikes were parked across Main Street, blocking any passage.

With less than ten feet to spare, the three boys slammed on their brakes and skidded into a spin. They whirled side-by-side in a complete circle and stopped inches from the wall of bikes. Drops of sweat rolled down Frank's rosy cheeks as Mike took in a deep breath of relief.

The crowd jumped to their feet and roared in a standing ovation.

Tom turned, a smile exploding across his face. "If that doesn't help them understand the beauty of our wheelie bikes, I don't know what will."

Whack! Mike slapped Frank across his back. "Nobody in this village can wheelie better than that."

"Yowch!" Frank scrunched his shoulders up into the bottom of his neck. "Let's find a spot in front of the stage."

A loud shriek screeched through the group of speakers, piercing the boys' eardrums. A low, brassy voice announced, "Our village mayor is here to open tonight's events. Introducing, Mayor Muff."

"Give it some gas! It's time to collect the cash!" shouted Tom as he raced by his friends.

"Feeling So Cool"
John W. Nassivera & Alan Dunham

The crowd paid tribute to their ride,
Tom's heart pounded with great pride,
The mayor bounced to the stage with a grin.
He wrenched the mic up to his chin,
Neighbors clapped for adoration,
acceptance, respect, and cooperation.
Come on, make it fast,
Come on, make it last.

I'm feeling so cool, how about you?
I'm feeling so cool, how about you?
I'm feeling so cool, how about you?

The crowd sung with a rock-n-roll beat,
Their song echoed up and down Main Street,
Tom's face gleamed with a glow of yellow.
He nudged his friend with an elbow,
Red and blue flashed like lightning,
Seeing the Grand Marshall is so exciting!
Come on, let's laugh,
Come on, let this feeling last.

I'm feeling so cool, how about you?
I'm feeling so cool, how about you?
I'm feeling so cool, how about you?
I'm feeling so cool, how about you?
I'm feeling so cool, how about you?
I'm feeling so cool, how about you?

The engine rumbled like thunder,
Fans gave a welcome and ponder,
Susanne in a floral sun dress.
She smiles just like a princess,
Rises above her tragic fall,

John W. Nassivera

Strong enough to break down any wall.
Susanne leaned in from her seat,
Proudly read from her prepared sheet,
When you lend a hand to patch the torn.
A rose blooms above its sharp thorns,
It's a choice to sing with a new voice,
My sisters and brothers hold hands and rejoice.
Come on, make it fast,
Come on, make it last.

I'm feeling so cool, how about you?
I'm feeling so cool, how about you?
I'm feeling so cool, how about you?
I'm feeling so cool, how about you?
I'm feeling so cool, how about you?
I'm feeling so cool, how about you?

I'm feeling so cool...
How about you...
I'm feeling so cool...
I'm feeling so cool...

The Cannon in The Park by Kendall McKernon

Chapter 14

Please Give a Warm Welcome

The sixty-seven bicyclists stood bunched together shoulder-to-shoulder surrounding the stairs to the bandstand. Mayor Muff bounced up the steps and slowly walked across the front of the stage. He waved, shook hands, and even stopped to kiss a baby. Mayor Muff then sauntered to the center of the stage and wrenched the mic upward below his chin. The applause quieted to a silence.

"For the second time today, that was some entrance." The Mayor pointed to the stairs at Tom, Mike, and Frank.

The crowd paid tribute to the boys' acrobatic show with shouts, laughter, and smiles.

The Mayor motioned the villagers silent. "Every year, we take time to come together as a community to celebrate the founding of our great village we call home."

Paradegoers of all ages, races, and faiths reached out to each other and stood tall.

"We accept our differences, for those differences are the special talents that will conquer the challenges and struggles we face as a community." He clasped his hands together and waved them over his head. "Most importantly, this is a time to promote a spirit of acceptance, respect, and cooperation, so that our faith and hope for the future grows as one."

Neighbors raised their clasped hands above their heads and cheered in unity.

The mayor smiled and said, "Is everyone ready to have some fun?"

The crowd screamed in unity, "Yes!"

Mayor Muff pointed across the park past the old cannon toward Maple Street. "We have live music from our local Music Hall." He threw his other hand out to the fire barn. "Arts & crafts, carnival rides, a farmers' market, a grilled chicken barbeque, and so much more."

The roar of the crowd echoed off the buildings surrounding the park.

"First, let me introduce you to this year's Grand Marshal," the Mayor said.

Tom gave Mike a soft nudge to the ribcage with his elbow and said, "This is what I've been waiting for."

A police siren echoed out of sight from the bottom of River Street Hill. Beams of red and blue light flashed like lightning, illuminating white, puffy clouds that floated in the sky. The hum of the engine rumbled like approaching thunder over the knoll onto Main Street. The siren screamed, *Woo-woo-woo-weeeooooeee*, as the car slowed to a stop behind the bandstand. The police chief and three officers jumped out and huddled together around the rear passenger side.

Tom restlessly fidgeted back-and-forth and danced in place, antsy for the contest results.

Mike looked to Tom, laughed, and said, "You better hold it. There's no bathroom close by."

"You're funnier than a barrel of monkeys," Tom said.

All four officers marched in a square formation from behind the bandstand, disappeared into the crowd of bicycle contestants, and emerged on the first step. Their shoes tapped with a rhythmic beat up the steps and across the stage.

"Squad halt, right turn, attention," commanded the police chief. The squad of officers stood, facing the crowd.

The park became completely quiet. Mayor Muff held his hand open to the officers and said, "Everyone, please give a warm welcome to this year's Grand Marshal."

The officers separated to the four corners of the stage and revealed a petite, brown-haired girl dressed in a beautiful floral lavender sun dress. The bottom of the dress ruffled into a bell shape, and its lace-covered sleeves stopped at her elbows. White silk gloves stretched upward over the length of her forearms. Silver buckles reflected the glossy shine cast from her black patent leather shoes, and her hair was twisted into a bun on top of her head.

"Our own beautiful princess and fifth grader at Margret Murphy Elementary School, Susanne E."

The crowd whistled, clapped, and cheered.

Mayor Muff waved the crowd to silence and continued his introduction. "Today, we honor one of our own, who lives a life of courage, fights for the happiness of others, and is forever giving," he said. "Although she is a little over four feet tall, she rises above us all in her determination to make our village a better place for you and me."

Tom, Mike, and Frank joined the bicyclists and their neighbors in clapping. Susanne stood center stage with a bright smile and waved her gloved hands to the townspeople.

The police chief pushed a wheelchair from the back of the stage. He carefully parked it behind Susanne while two other officers marched to her sides. The officers gently grasped her elbows and tenderly lowered her into the chair. Susanne looked up to each officer with affection and bowed her head with appreciation.

The park became silent.

Susanne leaned into the mic from her chair and read from a piece of paper she had prepared, "I thank every member of the community for this privilege to serve our village as Grand Marshal today. It is with great pleasure that I sit here with you and offer my appreciation and gratitude for the work you have done, are doing, and will continue to do in helping our neighbors."

She paused and looked up from the paper she was reading. "We can all make another person's life better. We can do it at any time. It's simply a matter of choice."

Tom's face reddened, and a warmth flooded through his earlobes. He looked away from Mike and Frank to hide his embarrassment. Guilt from his selfish impatience lumped in his throat.

Mayor Muff stepped back onto the stage, lightly tapped the mic twice, and said, "Our Susanne's beauty shines as an example of making that choice. She has courageously fought an ongoing battle to improve her health since her tragic accident as an infant." Mayor Muff folded his hands together and smiled down at Susanne. "This ongoing fight has never interfered with her heroic choice to always put the people around her first. The beauty of every rose rises above the sharpness of its thorns." He threw both arms out in front of the mic and pointed out at the crowd. "So, we ask everyone to join Susanne E's latest efforts to support our local food pantry by donating one can of food during this celebration."

Turning back, the Mayor opened both hands. "We thank Susanne for her continued service, and together, we will make our village a place we can all call home."

The townspeople stood to their feet.

Mayor Muff concluded, "To quote Susanne, 'Let's Show the Love.'"

The crowd raised their hands and voices in appreciation for Susanne. The villagers cheered for ten long seconds as Susanne E. was escorted by the officers to the side of the stage.

The police chief and officers marched to center stage and escorted the mayor down the steps to his seat. A hush fell over the park.

"Drum Roll Please"
John W. Nassivera, Albert Bouchard, David Hirschberg

A black mustache and Mutton chops
A drummer, a smash, a rhythm bomb drops
across a crash and two hanging toms
Tom crossed his fingers without any qualms

Drum roll, drum roll, drum roll please

Mr. B yelled into the mic, that was a blast
And now for the bike that best honors the past
A judge wearing a flowing chiffon gown
Blew her daughter a kiss while looking down

Drum roll, drum roll, drum roll please

And now the bike that celebrates the present
Ears perked up and the park became silent
The Schwinn Roadster boomed from the speakers
Sally raced right out of her sneakers

Drum roll, drum roll, drum roll please

A third contestant represents the future
We have a tie, three bikes that are super
Mr. B looked to the judges to see who had scored
The boys rushed the stage in search reward

Drum roll, drum roll, drum roll please

Where did you get the design for that crazy sprocket
Tom pulled a crumpled paper out from his pocket
The suspense of who will win grew bigger and bigger
Remember there can only be one winner
Drum roll, drum roll, drum roll please
Oh Yeah...

116

Chapter 15

Drum Roll, Please

A local musician with long, thick sideburns connected by a bushy, black mustache nosily clip-clopped across the stage wearing leather sandals. His blue jeans bellbottoms swished and swooshed with each step until the man flopped onto a stool behind the drum set. His lengthy, spindly fingers lifted two sticks from the hat of the snare drum. The knobby toes of his right foot poked out beneath a leather strap and stomped the foot-pedal, thumping the base drum. The drummer swiveled from the right side of the set and banged rhythmic thuds across the two hanging toms, a snare, a hi-hat, a ride cymbal, and a splash cymbal. He then ended with a single smash to the crash cymbal. The crowd became so quiet that they could hear a pin drop.

Mr. B walked to the center of the stage with Mrs. Fisher on his left and Mr. Irish on his right side. He adjusted the mic a little below his chin and said, "Are you ready to find out the winner?"

The crowd jumped to their feet.

Dressed in a red RPI College sweatshirt, Mr. Irish, an engineer by profession, stepped up to the mic. "The judging was exceptionally difficult this year," he said. "There were seventy different entries, the largest number of contestants to ever compete."

The bicyclists and their fans roared with excitement.

Mrs. Fisher, wearing a midnight blue empire silhouette gown and white gloves, stepped up to the mic. Her strawberry red hair shimmered under the spotlights. "We are now ready to announce the top three contenders." She handed a single envelope to Mr. B.

Mr. B leaned into the microphone and announced, "The bicycle that best honors the past is…" He turned back to the drummer and said, "Drum roll, please."

The percussionist rattled the heads of his drumsticks across the snare drum and ended on the splash cymbal. *Bum-brrum- brrrum-rat-a-tat-tat-badum-tish.*

Mr. B tore the envelope open, removed a card, looked out over the silent crowd, and paused for a quiet count of three.

"The 1930's Colson Flyer" roared from the wall of speakers and echoed off the buildings surrounding the park.

The crowd cheered as a twenty-eight-year-old mother jumped up and down with her three children. She hugged each of her boys and raced the

Colson up onto the stage. She made two brief stops on her way to the microphone, each time trembling and screaming her elation.

Tom dropped his head and kicked his foot into the grass.

Mr. B greeted the woman at center stage. "Tell us about your bike."

The mom squirmed with excitement and squeezed her hands to her face. She let go, her cheeks flushed red, and she said, "This is a Colson Flyer. It belongs to my father-in-law. This bike is not made any more and is a true antique."

"Fifty dollars is a lot of money. What will you do with all that money if you win first prize?" Mr. B asked.

Her three children, ages two, three, and five, ran up onto the stage and clung to her legs. The boys' mom gently touched and stroked her fingers through the eldest son's silky hair. Her eyes twinkled down with love as she nestled the children tightly to her thighs.

"These three little ones are growing right out of their clothes every few months. Fifty dollars will help fill the closet and my refrigerator."

The crowd cheered as Mr. Irish escorted the woman from the mic and positioned the mom and children off to the side. She gently nudged her nose to the top of her children's heads as she embraced them in one big hug.

Mrs. Fisher sauntered across the stage in her long, flowing chiffon gown and handed Mr. B the second envelope.

"The beautiful Mrs. Fisher," Mr. B said, pointing. "Let's give her a big round of applause, people."

The crowd slapped their hands together.

"That's my mom!" shouted a young, blonde girl, wearing a daisy yellow-colored party dress, from the third row.

The crowd cheered as Mrs. Fisher smiled and waved down from the stage to her daughter.

"Love you, Cathy." Mrs. Fisher blew her daughter a kiss, passed the envelope, and walked across the stage.

"The bicycle that best celebrates the present is…" Mr. B said.

The drummer beat his snare while Mr. B tore the envelope open, pulled the card out, and silently counted to three.

"The Schwinn Roadster" boomed from the speakers and echoed down Main Street.

The crowd cheered as Sally Smite raced the Schwinn up onto the stage and parked it next to Mr. B.

Frank hollered over the applause to Tom and Mike, "Sally wins every time she enters a contest. We don't stand a chance."

Mr. B asked, "Tell me about your bike and what you'll do if you win first prize."

"My dad bought me this bike just for this contest." Sally looked out at the crowd with a smile. "It won first place during this year's major bike manufactures' 100-yard dash competition."

"Now that's impressive," Mr. B said. "You mean to tell me that this bike beat the Norman Company and Colson Company for the fastest bike of the year?"

"That's right. Some people say it's the fastest bike in the world." Sally pointed down and smirked. "Just ask those three boys. They'll tell you how fast my Roadster is."

Tom whispered, "Cheater."

"Fifty dollars is a lot of cash," Mr. B said. "Do you have any plans for that money if you win?"

"My dad won a bike contest when he was my age, and he gave his bike to a friend who couldn't afford one," Sally said. She pulled the mic from Mr. B and held it to her mouth. "Just like my Dad, I'll give the money to charity." Sally waved to the crowd, turned back to Mr. B, and said loud and clear for the whole park to hear, "I'll tell you what charity after you announce the winner." She handed the mic back.

"Wow! That's being confident," Mr. B said.

"There's still one competitor to be announced," Frank said. "It's not over."

"This is our last chance. Cross your fingers." Tom crossed his fingers, arms, legs, and even two of his toes. He stared down at his feet and broke into a cold sweat.

"The third time's the charm." Frank gave a reassuring pat to Tom's shoulder.

"Our third contestant, representing a look towards the future, is…" Mr. B said.

Tom continued to stare down at his sneakers. Drops of moisture formed on his forehead, and his stomach growled as loud as the drum roll.

Bum-brrum- brrrum-rat-a-tat-tat-badum-tish, crashed the cymbal.

121

Mike tapped Tom's shoulder with a peppy *pat-ta-tap-tap* and said, "Don't sweat it."

Mr. B pulled the card from the envelope.

Tom slowly lifted his head and glanced out over the park. Every villager was crammed into the center of town, shoulder-to-shoulder, with every eye focused on the stage.

"Our third contender to have the opportunity to win a grand prize of fifty dollars is…." Mr. B paused, and a look of disbelief fell across his face. "Oh, this is unusual." He silently showed the card to Mr. Irish and whispered, "This can't be right."

Mr. Irish cupped his hand, covered his mouth from the crowd, and spoke into the back of Mr. B's ear.

A silence fell over the cyclists and spread throughout the crowd.

Mr. B held the card out at an arm's length, squinted, and read, "The Renegade."

Mike jumped two feet into the air, threw several fist pumps, and shouted, "Yes! Yes! Yes!" A smile beamed across his face as he turned to his friends.

The crowd cheered.

Mr. B shouted into the mic, "That's not all, folks." He paused, and the crowd became silent, except for Mike's "Woo-hoos" and "Oh, yeahs."

Mike squeezed Frank into a bear hug and squished a long whistling, rattling wheeze from Frank's lungs.

Mr. B announced, "We have a tie, with the Blue Lightning."

Frank's chin fell to his chest, and he blurted out, "What? You have to be kidding me!" He clutched Mike's arms and mushed his biceps to the bone. "I've never won anything!"

"Ow, that hurts." Mike's face cringed as he flinched. "When did you get super strength?"

The two friends jumped in each other's arms as the crowd cheered. Tom turned from the stage and began to quietly slither away through the bicyclists. Mike caught a glance of Tom slumped over and disheartened. He tapped Frank on the shoulder, and the two boys reached out.

"There's still more," shouted Mr. B.

The crowd "Oohed" and "Aahed."

Mr. B paused again, and the park became silent once more.

"The Sting-Ray!" bellowed from the wall of speakers.

Tom jumped into his friend's arms. Frank stumbled, and then they all tumbled to the ground as a human ball and rolled onto their backs side-by-side.

Tom grinned and said, "Project J-38."

Mr. B said into the mic over the roar of the crowd, "Why don't you boys stop monkeying around and bring your bikes up onto the stage?"

Mike was first to run his bike onto the stage, followed by Tom, and then Frank. Mr. Irish directed them to the center and positioned them and their bikes side-by-side.

"These three bikes are almost as crazy looking as those shirts you're wearing," Mr. B said. "What can you tell us about your bikes?"

Tom stepped to the mic and said, "These three bikes are called wheelie bikes, or banana bikes, or Spyder bikes. The coolest thing about our three bikes is that our six hands made them from old bicycle parts in our garages."

Mr. Irish looked the bikes up and down. He then reviewed his notes on the clipboard. "You boys are quite the engineers. Where did you get the design plans?"

Tom pulled a crumpled piece of paper from his jeans pocket and handed it to Mr. Irish. "I sketched it on this flyer."

Mr. Irish unraveled the paper, "Amazing."

Mr. B asked, "So, tell us what you three are going to do if you win the cash prize."

Tom grabbed the microphone and said, "Buy a spanking new Project J-38."

"I'm going to buy barbells and dumbbells," Mike said. "Watch out Superman, here I come."

Frank jumped onto the mic, pointed out across the park at an ice cream vendor, and said, "The first thing I'm going to do is buy a Creamsicle from that guy over there."

The crowd roared with laughter.

Mr. B took the mic, extended his left arm toward the finalists, and announced, "There you have it: our three, I mean five, contenders for the grand prize. However, there can only be one winner."

Tom looked out with a smile that stretched from ear to ear. He had worked hard for six long months and now stood on stage, front and center. His mother's voice rang inside his head, *It's what you do that lifts you up.*

"Now, for the moment we've all been waiting for," announced Mr. B. "Here to award this year's Grand Prize to the winner of the bicycle competition is the Grand Marshal, Susanne E."

Susanne's white gloves gently clenched the two large tires beneath the arms of the wheelchair and thrust downward. Her petite frame rolled across the stage. The crowd cheered as she braked to a stop next to the microphone. To her left stood Mike, Tom, and Frank. On her right stood Sally and the mother with her three children.

"Susanne has been in that wheelchair since she fell out of the second-floor window as a baby," Frank said to his friends.

"That chair doesn't slow her down," Mike said. "She's involved in everything. She played on my summer basketball team."

Tom spoke out of the side of his mouth, "She's wicked smart. She's the best reader in my reading plus group. She's only in fifth grade."

Susanne wheeled to the front of the stage, locked the brakes, and slowly pushed herself upwards. "Throughout our village, you will see many metal trash cans painted by my classmates into Tender Loving Cans." She pointed to a blue can next to the stage. "I ask that you 'Show the Love' to our neighbors by lending a hand with a can. When you place a can of food in the TLCan, you will receive a happy heart."

Mike whispered to Tom and Frank, "Where did I hear that before?"

"What's that?" whispered Frank.

"Lend a hand with a can," Mike said.

The three boys stared into each other's eyes, remembering at the exact same time.

The boy's jaws dropped as they said, "Uh, oh."

"Oh, yes," Tom gasped in horror with his mouth wide open. "What if the judges find out?"

Frank clutched the sleeve of Tom's T-shirt and said, "It was a mistake. I swear."

Mike shrugged his shoulders and held both palms open at his sides. "It's creamed corn. That messy slop is nasty." Mike's shoulders rolled upwards. "Nobody eats that disgusting yellow porridge."

"That's not the point," whispered Tom. He pulled the two friends downwards by their neckbands. "We took something that didn't belong to us. That's wrong."

"It was an honest mistake," Frank said. "The judges will understand."

Mike's face scrunched up, pulling the corners of his mouth upwards into a snide grin. "Are you kidding me?" he said. "We almost ran Mr. B over, Tom didn't get his hair cut, and now we stole our entry fee from the poor."

Tom glanced over his shoulder to the front of the stage. Susanne E. turned the wheelchair back toward the microphone, and their eyes stared into each other's. Tom quickly looked away, hiding his head back into the huddle of friends.

"Time is running out; we have to think of something fast," Tom said.

Mike peeked over Tom's shoulder and then quickly ducked back into the huddle. "She's rolling this way."

"The Winner Is"
John W. Nassivera & Alan Dunham

Tom stood on stage with his bike in first gear
A smile stretching ear to ear
The moment we've been waiting for
Suzanne rolled across the floor
She said come on lend a hand with a can
There's a monkey wrench in our plan
Boys said, what's all the fuss
Those cans didn't belong to us

We've gotta keep moving along
We've gotta win this race
We've gotta keep moving along
We've gotta win this race
We've gotta keep moving along
And the winner is...

Cream corn makes my grandpa gassy
The messy slop is downright nasty
Pulled the boys by their neckbands
What if the judges don't understand
The crowd gasped, moaned and groaned and grumbled
That can't be, the town rumbled
Watching the swirling wheels
Tom staggered back on his heels

We've gotta keep moving along
We've gotta win this race
We've gotta keep moving along
We've gotta win this race
We've gotta keep moving along
And the winner is...
We've gotta keep moving along
We've gotta win this race
We've gotta keep moving along

127

We've gotta win this race
We've gotta keep moving along
And the winner is...

Susanne wheelied on her rear tires
The crowd trumpet that inspires
We can still fix this
We could win out of five finalists
Held the envelope by her head
Susanne tore it open and read
Pounding his chest like King Kong
Tom won, get ready for a song

We've gotta keep moving along
We've gotta win this race
We've gotta keep moving along
We've gotta win this race
We've gotta keep moving along
And the winner is...
We've gotta keep moving along
We've gotta win this race
We've gotta keep moving along
We've gotta win this race
We've gotta keep moving along
And the winner is...
The winner is...
The winner is...

Village Facades by Kendall McKernon

Chapter 16

The Winner Is...

The crowd gasped and then grumbled. Frank peeked from behind Mike's rainbow splotched T-shirt and reported, "Everyone is pointing at the stage."

Tom blushed bright red and said, "They must know." He hastily slithered behind Mike and Frank and ducked out of sight.

Shouts of "That can't be" and "No Way" erupted from the crowd.

Tom peered out around Frank and witnessed the audience looking in his direction. He ducked back behind the boys, and a roar erupted throughout the park. He swiveled to the other side and peeked around Mike's shoulder.

"I don't believe it," Tom said.

The heels of Susanne's shinny shoes whished through the air above the microphone as her hair bun whisked across the floor. She wheelied in a circle, faster and faster, whirling and twirling.

Tom tilted back on his heels, dizzy from watching the swirling wheelie. He suddenly lost his footing and clutched at his two friends in an attempt to break his fall. Mike and Frank braced their bodies, snatched Tom by the wrist, and pulled him flat on his feet. The three gazed with gaping eyes.

Susanne E. thrusted both tires forward in unison, jetting across the stage in a spectacular wheelie.

Tom's head dropped to Mike's hip. His eyes bulged from their sockets. The chair suddenly veered left, wheelied to center stage, and stopped in front of the mic. Susanne tittered back-and-forth on the rear tires, and the two front wheels hovered above the mic.

The crowd stood and cheered.

Susanne dropped the front tires, thwacking the stage with a thunderous boom, which silenced the crowd.

"Did you see that? Now, that's a wheelie!" trumpeted from the wall of speakers lining the back of the stage. Susanne pointed directly at the boys, yelling, "Who's the boss?"

The crowd exploded into a roar, and Tom took it as a cue to push his way from behind Mike and Frank. The three boys smiled, pointed back at Susanne, and hollered, "You're the BOSS!"

Susanne turned back to the crowd and adjusted her posture in the wheelchair.

"She doesn't know," Tom said out of the side of his mouth. "We still have time to fix this."

Mrs. Fisher walked to the center of the stage and stepped to the microphone. "Before we announced the winner of this year's contest, we have a special presentation from one of our neighbors." Mrs. Fisher opened her arms, welcoming the guest presenter.

A man in his late forties with golden blonde, wavy hair strutted onto the stage elegantly dressed in a blue business suit highlighted by a red tie. He had a swagger of confidence and success. He stood poised with perfect posture at six feet and four inches tall and calmly adjusted the cufflinks at the end of each shirt sleeve.

The crowd was silent.

"Good evening," greeted the man. "My name is Mr. Smite."

The crowd remained silent.

He grasped the lapels of his jacket with both hands and stood as proud as a peacock. Mr. Smite extended his hand out to Mr. B and presented him with an envelope. "I would like to make a donation to the school's Reading is Fun Program."

The villagers broke their silence with a round of applause.

Mr. Smite bent into Mr. B's ear and said with a smile, "Second place wasn't half bad." He turned, took three steps to his daughter, and held Sally in his arms.

Sally looked up into her dad's eyes and said, "I'm going to win, just like you did."

Mr. Smite hugged his daughter and said, "Do the best you can." He kissed her on the forehead.

"Mr. Smite thinks money can buy anything." Mike turned to Tom and said under his breath, "Did he pay you to hang out with Sally?"

"I've never met Mr. Smite." Tom scratched his head.

Frank reached out and grabbed Tom's arm. "What happen between you two?"

Susanne's dainty voice announced, "OK people, now for the moment our finalists have all been waiting for. The bicycle that wins third place is…" She turned back to the drummer and said, "Drum roll, please."

The percussionist rattled, *Bum-brrum- brrrum-rat-a-tat-tat-badum-tish.*

Susanne tore the envelope open, removed a card, and read, "The 1930's Colson Flyer."

The mom of three took a slight step forward and waved out to the crowd.

The three boys and Sally lined up at the front of the stage side-by-side. Sally's open hand rested an inch from Tom's.

Susanne held the winning envelope above her head and said, "Now, for the winner of this year's bike contest." She turned to the back of the stage and requested, "Drum roll, please."

Sweat beaded across Tom's forehead beneath his wavy bangs. He wavered over his ankles, dithered, and softly grasped Sally's hand.

Bum-brrum- brrrum-rat-a-tat-tat-badum-tish.

Sally slapped Tom's hand away without breaking her stare out over the crowed park.

Tom shook the sting from his hand.

132

Susanne tore the envelope open, removed a card, and paused to look up at the crowd.

"The Sting-Ray!"

Tom pounded his chest like King Kong and yelled out in victory, "AwwwAAA!"

Mike and Frank pounced onto his back, screaming in triumph. The three plummeted to the floor and playfully scuffled. Mike threw a headlock on Tom while Frank curled his third finger and twisted several celebratory nuggies on Tom's noggin. The boys rolled onto the disc-shaped base, swirling the microphone through the air.

Mr. B took a giant step over the boys, caught the mic as it spun toward the floor, and announced to the crowd, "That concludes this year's contest, but the party has just begun. The bazaar is now open at Paris Park."

The boys rolled over Mr. B's foot, and his mouth twisted into a grimace. He pulled his foot from beneath the pile and said, "Please be back by dusk. We'll have the Music Hall Band performing live, right here in Juckett Park."

The roadies rushed onto the stage as the crowd emptied the park. A roadie in his early twenties hauled a bundle of electrical cords lassoed around his neck and shoulders up the stairs. He flipped the bundle over his long hair into a heap onto the floor next to the boys. The friends glanced up.

The roadie said with a smile, "Bands make it rock. Roadies make it roll."

Mike turned to Tom and said, "Hey, let's roll over to the bazaar."

"Great idea," Frank said. "We better hurry before all the barbeque chicken gets eaten. I'm starving."

Mike and Frank dashed for the stairs, zigging to the right, zagging to the left, and snaking through a maze of roadies carrying cables, speakers, microphones, and instruments in a race to set up the stage for the concert.

Frank called up from the bottom step, "Hey, champ."

Tom glanced down and noticed one of Susanne's TLCans stationed a few feet from the stairs. It had been painted sky-blue, and the yellow print read, "Lend a helping hand with a can."

"Hey, champ," Frank said once again. "Let's go!"

Tom pushed his bangs to the side and asked, "Were there any words painted on that orange can?"

"I didn't notice any." Mike sat on his bike, turned back to Frank, and asked, "Did you see any words painted on the can?"

"Nope," Frank said. "Why?"

Tom scratched his head and said, "What if the words, 'Lend a helping hand' weren't painted on the can?"

Frank pointed and twirled his left index finger next to his temple. "That's wishful thinking," he said, puffing his cheeks and squeezing his lips into a kooky twist.

Mike looked Tom straight in the eyes with a scrunched-up face.

"You're right." Tom grasped his chin, kneaded it like dough, and stared off into space. "We have to decide how we're going to tell Mr. B and do it fast."

Frank's stomach grumbled, and he moaned, "I can't think on an empty stomach."

Tom turned to his friends and smiled. "Bring me back a Creamsicle." He took three steps across the stage. "Hurry back."

"You got it, champ," Frank said, pedaling off beside Mike to the bazaar.

Tom's heart fluttered in his chest as he paced back-and-forth across the front of the stage. "How am I going to tell Mr. B the truth?" he asked himself out loud as he took two long strides to the top of the stairs and walked down. He stopped and peered at the donations of canned goods piled halfway up the container.

Bobby popped up from behind the sky-blue Tender Loving Can.

Tom jumped back, clasping his hand over his heart. His blood ran cold, and a chill ran through his bones as he screeched, "You freaked me out."

Bobby smiled and gurgled a chuckle from the back of his throat as he sneered over the top of the can.

There was something about the sinister, murmuring giggle that rubbed Tom the wrong way. "How long have you been hiding behind that can?"

Bobby said, "Long enough."

"Head in a Haze"
John W. Nassivera & Alan Dunham

On the stage snaking through a maze
Not seeing clearly, head in a haze
Winning first prize gave a stinging cut
A wrong feeling deep down in the gut

A rust-pitted bike rolls to a stop
Giving to others, when they don't got
That woman's struggles are not hers alone
Rise to your feet, step down from the throne

Rock me with the answer I need
Roll me to a field of dreams
Not to the beat of the same old tune
Searching high and low for the perfect pitch
Giving is always the right gift
Bands make it rock, Roadies make it roll
Write me a song, that's music to the soul

Moan and groan in search for the right tone
Blood running cold, chilling to the bone
Hand clutching a quietly beating heart
Making the right choice sets us apart

Reach into the envelope and draw lots
A lighthearted voice stirs drowning thoughts
A good harmony brings us together
Through all seasons and all kinds of weather

Rock me with the answer I need
Roll me to a field of dreams
Not to the beat of the same old tune
Searching high and low for the perfect pitch
Giving is always the right gift
Bands make it rock, Roadies make it roll

Chain Links

Write me a song, that's music to the soul

Rock me with the answer I need
Roll me to a field of dreams
Not to the beat of the same old tune
But music for the soul...
Searching high and low for the perfect pitch
Giving is always the right gift
Bands make it rock, Roadies make it roll
Write me a song, that's music to the soul

Chapter 17

Fist of Fifty

Bobby jetted into the crowd and disappeared from sight.

"Hey, Tom. Are you forgetting something?" Mr. B asked from the stage.

A shiver raced up Tom's spine, restricting his breathing and causing him to squeak like a mouse.

"What's wrong? The cat got your tongue?" Mr. B waved a bulging white envelope. The glued seams barely held the #10 envelope sealed.

Tom slowly walked up the stairs, stopping on each step. His ears pinged to the pulsing of his heart throbbing as if it was going to jump out of his chest.

"Congratulations." Mr. B slapped the envelope of cash against the palm of Tom's open hand. "Your hard work earned the respect of the judges."

Tom clutched the prize close to his chest in an ironclad grip.

"So, tell me about this new bike you mentioned on stage," Mr. B asked.

Tom half-smiled, "It's the newest thing out there, charcoal black, sporty, blistering fast; it's the fastest bike on the planet." He gasped a deep long breath.

Mr. B giggled and asked, "Fastest on the planet?"

"Supersonic fast," Tom said, springing from his slouch.

Mr. B took a step back and asked, "Faster than the Schwinn Roadster?"

"No question!" Tom's fingers clasped around his thumb into fist. "That bike Sally showed doesn't stand a chance."

Mr. B laughed and said with a smile, "That sounds like a challenge."

"Any day of the week," Tom said with a stern frown. "I'm always ready for a fair-and-square race." He slapped the envelope of cash against his chest. "I can't wait to buy that bike and beat the pants off Sally in front of the whole school."

"I hope you give a little thought about helping our neighbors before deciding what to do with all that money." Mr. B looked down at the Sting Ray. "Some of our neighbors could get by with a little help from a friend." He slowly turned back and gently rested his hand on Tom's shoulders. "Whatever you do, have fun."

"Oh, I'm going to have fun flying by Sally with blistering speed," Tom said. "See you Monday at school."

Tom stomped across the front of the stage and treaded heavily down the stairs. He flopped down on the banana seat, arched back into the sissy bar, and gazed at the stack of dollar bills splitting the envelope open at the corners. He jammed his index finger between the bills and the gummed seal. The edge of the paper delivered a stinging paper cut to his finger as he tore the seal open. A dab of blood smeared onto the first three dollars as he pulled bill after bill from the never-ending stack and counted, "Twenty-eight, twenty-nine, thirty."

"Congratulations!" a woman's voice said.

Tom clutched his winnings in both hands and peered upward. A rust-pitted bicycle rolled to a stop beside him. It was the Colson Flyer. The mom from the contest smiled as she clenched the handlebars. Her three children clung to the fabric of her blouse and pants legs.

The mother said with a soft, gentle tone, "Who wants to help me pick out the perfect place on the lawn to spread out the blanket before Grandpa gets back?"

The children excitedly jumped up and down, waved their hands above their heads, and shouted, "Me, me, me!" The three then skipped off, holding hands.

The woman smiled at Tom and said, "Your bike is unusual! My father-in-law would love to have a bicycle like that in his collection."

"Over here. Over here, mom," the eldest child shouted while standing near the stage.

The other two children ran back, surrounded their mother, and nudged her away. The woman played a game of peek-a-boo with a smile as she struggled to spread the blanket on the grass.

Tom stuffed the envelope down the front of his shirt, dismounted the Sting Ray, and strolled to the front of the bandstand. "You look like you could use some help," Tom said.

The two grabbed the four corners in their hands, held tight, and threw the blanket above their heads. A light breeze blew upwards, opening the blanket like a parachute. The three children raced back-and-forth beneath the chute as it slowly floated downward. The eldest boy crawled from under the blanket as it settled to the grass. He jumped to his feet, and all three children rolled and tumbled to the center. The wrestling match began.

The mom smiled across the blanket at Tom and said, "That was very kind of you. Thank you."

Tom jogged back to his bike and flopped onto the banana seat. "You're welcome. Enjoy the concert," he replied. Tom arched back against the sissy bar, stretched his arms upward to the sky, and contently yawned. He felt pleased with himself as he reached into the envelope and separated the pile of one-dollar bills in half. The bills shuffled from each hand, interweaving below his thumbs. His fingers arched the pile upward into a bridge and pushed the two stacks together as one. Tom dealt the bills into separate piles of ten.

The three children roll over their mother's feet as she pulled three cans from a wire basket hanging from the front handlebars of the Colson. She bent down and handed each child a can of soup.

"Brendan, take your brothers to the stairs and help them drop the chicken soup into the big blue can."

The children raced from the blanket with the cans in their hands. Brendan arrived at the stairs first and waited for his brothers. He reached above the rim and dropped the can, and then helped his brothers by lifting each of them up. One after the other, they released their cans, and watched them fall into the blue barrel. The younger brothers rollicked back to their mom, tee-heeing as Brendan flitted their ear lobes with a snap of his finger.

Tom twist and turned to the end of the banana seat. He pictured his mother's smile the last three mornings as she served him and his family oatmeal.

Chapter 18

If Not You, Then Who?

Tom rubbed his fingers across the edge of the dollar bills and lost count at twenty when his mind drifted. *I should have been happy to eat oatmeal, even though it was the third day in a row.* Tom's throat tightened. "Eight, nine, ten," muttered out of his mouth. His thoughts wandered to Sally waiting on the corner of Coleman Avenue. His chest knotted up, pulling his shoulders forward into a slump. "I never said sorry to Sally."

A jolly, lighthearted voice interrupted his sorrowful thoughts. "Dude, that tie-dyed shirt is hippy-dippy."

The long-haired customer from Emery's barbershop walked beside the bandstand and stopped next to the stairs, holding a tattered guitar case.

"Hey, bro. That's a handful of bread you got there," the musician said.

Tom stared at his fistful of cash. His chin fell, pulling his mouth open.

"What are you planning to do with all those greenbacks?" the musician asked.

"Oh, for the last six months, I've been daydreaming of riding a brand-new Project J-38 bike at jet speed to school," Tom said with a muffled voice. "But, now I'm not sure."

The musician's forehead wrinkled with a thought. "Daydreaming, daydreamer, day tripper," he said. "Hmm, sounds like a song I've heard."

Tom slumped down over the handlebars and moaned, "Uhmm…"

"What's got you all uptight?" the musician asked, walking up the stairs and stopping on the third step.

"I need to make a choice," Tom said. "I don't know what to do."

The young man smiled, "Sometimes, music provides me with the answer to my problems."

Tom lowered his head and stuffed the cash back into the envelope. "It was nice talking with you, but I have to figure this out."

The musician held his hand in the air with two fingers up in a "V." "Peace." He leaped over the last step, darted onto the stage, and hollered back, "All we need is LOVE."

Two young children raced around the fountain in the middle of the park, playing tag. A group of old men huddled around two elderly friends who were fiercely battling in a game of chess. Cyndi and the seven water gunners leaned against a huge oak tree and chattered like squirrels. A musician wearing an electric guitar was handed a cable jack by the last roadie. Suddenly, a high frequency *tweak* screeched from the speakers, broadcasting a signal for everyone to find their seats for the start of the show.

A white glove gave three sharp jerks to Tom's shirt. Tom's heart skipped a beat as his stomach tightened into a knot. A croaky "hey" choked from the bottom of his throat.

"Congratulations," Susanne said in an upbeat tone.

Tom's tongue felt swollen to five times its normal size. "Thank you," he mumbled from a half-smile.

"You must be proud about winning first prize," Susanne said, smiling up from her wheelchair. "You have to be wicked smart to design a bike that different."

Tom slumped into the banana seat.

"Something bothering you?" she asked. "Is there something I can help you with?"

Tom gulped and muttered, "Oh, no. Not at all."

"Tell me about this bike you want to buy."

"It's called the Project J-38." Tom leaned out between the handlebars and hung his head over the headlight.

"Project J-38 sounds like a name for shampoo or dish washing soap." Susanne said. "Sting-Ray is a much cooler name."

Tom rose off the seat to his feet. "You don't understand. It's this really cool wheelie bike made by a top engineer." His shoulders rolled back. "It has a sissy bar, banana seat, mag rear tire, and ape hanger handlebars." His face flushed red as he grabbed the handgrip of the Sting Ray and nervously twirled the ape hangers back and forth. "It has extended front forks and a super small wheelie tire in the front. Riding that bike to school means everything to me!"

Susanne asked, "Is it a 5-speed?"

Tom's glasses slid down to the tip of his nose. "No. Why?" He flopped back down on the banana seat.

She pointed at his bike and said, "That Project J-38 would surely lose a race against your 5-speed." Susanne rolled beside the Sting Ray.

Tom stared at the gear shift mounted on the Sting Ray. "Just this morning, I won a race by shifting into fifth gear." Tom sat up straight and tilted his head back. "You should have seen the faces on Mike and Frank as I sped by them." He threw a quick fist pump across the front of his body. "It was priceless!"

Susanne E. wheeled around the Sting Ray. She smiled up at Tom and said, "Everyone at school would be proud to ride this bike. It's one of a kind."

Tom stood straight as an arrow, straddled the banana seat, and said, "The Sting Ray, Renegade, and Blue Lightning are different from every bike in the contest today."

"Being different is what makes us special." She nudged her body to the front of the wheelchair. "Did you know that no two snowflakes are the same?"

"No. I once read that no two stars in the universe are exactly the same."

Susanne E. laughed. "I guess you can say being different is what makes the world go 'round."

The two laughed together out loud.

"I guess I'm not the only wicked smart one in the park today," Tom said with a smile. His smile quickly fell to a frown. A lump became lodged in his throat, and he gulped. "There's something I have to tell you."

"What's that?"

Tom paused with his eyes wide open, fixated on his sneakers. "Hmm," he hesitated as he leaned forward between the handlebars.

"What is it, Tom?"

"Uhmm… I was thinking. Uhmm…" Tom was buying time to build up the courage to tell Susanne about the creamed corn. "Did any of your classmates paint one of the cans orange?"

"Yes," Susanne said. "Tony and Christine painted their can orange." She held her index finger to her bottom lip and paused. "I think it was on Elm Street."

Susanne wheeled to the front of the Sting Ray and looked up into Tom's face. "Why?"

Tom took in a deep breath and sat straight up on his bicycle seat. "I think me and my friends made a mistake."

Susanne E. smiled and said, "How bad could it be? I'm sure you can fix it."

"Oh, he can fix it, alright," called out a familiar, snooty voice.

Sally stood beside the sky-blue can several yards away. She propped the yellow Roadster up on its kickstand, folded her arms across her chest, and stuck out her tongue.

"You can give me that fifty dollars you stole from me."

"Stole from you?" Tom snapped at Sally. "The only crime committed here today was you and your sidekick Bobby cheating during our race."

"You're such a sore loser," giggled Sally. "Isn't that right, Bobby?"

There was no response.

"Bobby, did you hear this namby-pamby whining about losing the race?" Sally tapped her left foot to the ground, waiting for his response.

There was no answer.

Chain Links

Tom spotted Bobby ten yards to his left, bent over the fountain and splashing water onto two boys that were half his age. The tots ran soaked and wet into a swell of people returning from the bazar. They bobbed and weaved against the current of concert goers, their sneakers squishing and sloshing as they cried out for their mothers.

"You done?" Sally shouted over at Bobby.

"Oh," Bobby said with his hands still splashing in the fountain. "That was fun."

Tom's shoulders tensed upward, and he turned his bike to go confront Sally and Bobby but hit a snag when his right pedal got hitched between the spokes of Susanne's left rear tire.

Tom asked, "Are you all right?"

Susanne was silent.

Tom slowly turned, fearing the worst, but there sat Susanne E. in her wheelchair, wearing a smile.

"Why are you smiling? I don't get it," Tom said, drooping his head. "Don't you want to smash those two?"

She rocked the wheels back and forth, releasing the pedal. "I can get mad and get bad if I want to."

Tom was silent for a second. He had heard his mother tell him a hundred billion times that getting mad never solved anything. A lump lodged in his throat, and he gulped, "Everyone I know would say something mean to Sally and Bobby."

Susanne turned and looked toward Sally and Bobby, who were more than ten feet away. "Does she look like she's wearing her happy face?"

147

Tom snickered and whispered, "Looks more like an upside-down smile to me."

"Yeah, that's not Sally's pretty look." Susanne giggled and bumped Tom's front tire with her wheelchair, joggling Tom's head upward. "Go say something nice."

Tom sighed as he looked over at Sally. "Ugh, I don't really want to."

Susanne said, "Change has to start with someone."

"You sound like my mom," Tom said. "Sally started it when she called me and my friend's bikes garbage." Tom's anger reddened his face. "Why me?"

"If not you, then who?" Susanne asked.

Tom's chin dropped onto his neck as he folded his arms across his chest.

Susanne pointed towards Sally and gently nudged Tom forward.

Sally waved Bobby to the stage and shouted, "Hurry over here and tell Susanne E. what you overheard."

Columbus Day in The Park by Kendall McKernon

Chapter 19

It's Our Secret

The stage lights blinked several times, signaling the last moments of preparation on the bandstand. The flow of families and friends walking from Paris Park had dwindled to a trickle. Open space to view the concert had become sparse and scattered. People squeezed together on park benches, bodies old and young wedged into folding beach chairs, and patches of multicolored blankets came together in a quilt over the green lawn.

Sally impatiently taped her foot, waiting for Bobby.

149

"Hey Tom! Over here," Frank yelled from the oak as he waved both hands in big circles.

Tom glanced at his friends, then back over at Sally. Bobby stood beside her, yakking away. "Let's forget about those two and join my friends to watch the concert," Tom said to Susanne.

"I hope Cyndi's platoon has run out of water." Susanne softly ran her fingers over her dress. "I'm not wearing a swimsuit."

"I think you're safe." Tom returned the smile and pointed both thumbs to his multicolor shirt. "I can guarantee they emptied their water guns earlier today."

Tom clutched the handlebars, leaned forward, and pushed into the maze of concert goers. The bike jerked to a stop before his second step. *What now?* Tom thought.

It was Susanne, who was holding the bottom of the sissy bar, and she pulled him to a stop.

"I thought we needed to hurry?" Tom asked.

Suanne pointed her thumb over her shoulder and said, "This may be your chance."

"Chance for what?" Tom spotted Sally and Bobby loitering next to the stage. Bobby bamboozled a second grader out of his last stick of bubblegum. "You're kidding!"

Susanne said. "What can it hurt to ask?"

Tom took a deep long breath and groaned, "You mean who can it hurt?" He shook his head, wagging his bangs back and forth, and moaned in despair. "I might as well throw myself under a moving train."

Susanne looked up with her gentle, contagious smile.

"Ugh," squirmed Tom. He looked away, but he couldn't fight the urge to smile back. "Okay. I'll do it."

He turned his bike around and wheeled back, stopping five feet from the steps of the stage. "Hey, Sally and Bobby. Do you guys want to join us for the concert?"

Sally looked back and forth through the crowded park, as if she was trying to find who Tom was asking to join him. She turned to Bobby and asked, "He can't be talking to us?"

Bobby chomped and chewed the stolen stick of gum. "Yeah, he's asking us."

Susanne rolled up to Tom and said into the back of his ear, "I don't think they heard you."

"Oh, they heard me," Tom faintly said out of the side of his mouth.

Susanne pulled her white gloves tightly over her fingers and said, "May I suggest that you get off your bike and ask them face-to-face?"

"Shucks," Tom grumbled, turning from Susanne. He slowly flopped off the bike and mumbled down to his feet as the rubber soles of his sneakers scuffed through the grass.

Bobby stepped in front of Sally, holding his hand outward against Tom's chest, and braced him to a stop. "That's far enough," Bobby said.

Tom bit down on his tongue to avoid shouting. The two stared angrily into each other's eyes as Tom said, "Remove your hand from my shirt."

Sally stood hidden behind Bobby and barked out her orders. "Ask him if he brought my fifty dollars."

Bobby stepped up to Tom's face, nose-to-nose. He jabbed his index finger into Tom's chest.

"Did you bring Sally's first-place prize money?" Bobby poked the tip of his finger into Tom's chest several more times. "You know she's the true winner."

Tom grabbed Bobby's finger and bent it back over his hand. Bobby dropped to one knee and begged Tom to stop.

"Ouch, ow, owie, youch, yow, yowch!" cried Bobby. "Stop, let go!"

Susanne E. wheeled up beside the boys and grasped Tom's wrist. "That's not a good start." She calmly pulled Tom's hand to his side.

Tom snarled, "He started it."

Susanne slid upright to the front of her seat and extended an open gloved hand to Sally. "We wanted to invite you to watch the concert with us."

Sally turned her head away, not able to exchange looks with Susanne.

Tom thought that he witnessed the corner of Sally's mouth slightly turning upward.

Suddenly, she turned back, shoving Suanne's white glove to the side. Sally lunged past the wheelchair, knocked Bobby to the side, and stepped up into Tom's mug. Her teeth gnashed as she said, "We've tried that." She stared into Tom's eyes.

"Why would we want to be friends with this cheater?" Bobby grumbled.

"I know you cheated. That's the only way you could have a chance of beating me," Sally said. "You wait and see. Bobby and I are going to report it to the judges."

Bobby rubbed his index finger and said, "Cheat, cheat, never beat."

"Why would we want to join a bunch of losers?" Sally pointed to the kids beneath the oak tree. "Why don't you go join your loser friends?"

"Yeah, start walking, you loser," Bobby said.

Tom looked away from Susanne, hoping he would come up with a way to tell Susanne about the orange TLCan before Sally did. "You can't say I didn't try." Tom kicked the kickstand up and walked away.

Susanne E. wheeled past Sally up behind Tom and said, "If at first you don't succeed, try again."

Tom grunted. "You don't know when to give up."

"I think we made Sally happy," Susanne said.

Tom stopped his bike. "Sally sure has a funny way of showing happiness. Let's go before things get any uglier."

Tom bobbed and weaved into the crowd. Susanne grappled with the clunky four wheels of her chair through the tightly packed masses of people. A bike propped upward on its kickstand barricaded their path to the tree.

"I don't want to discourage you." Tom arched up on the tip of his toes. He joggled his head side-to-side, looking for a clear route to his friends. "Time is ticking. Maybe we should park ourselves here for the concert."

Susanne huffed and puffed as she rolled closer to the barrier. "Plenty of things will block your path," she panted. "You can't let them stop you." She pushed onward, saying, "Let's keep moving."

As they approached the barricade, Tom took closer notice of the bike in the way. "Hey, that's the Colson Flyer."

Tom wheeled left around the rusty bike, and Susanne rolled to the right. She hollered over to Mrs. Emery as she passed the Colson, "Congratulations! Your bike is wonderful."

The mom sat on the blanket and grinned as her three children restlessly climbed one-by-one over her shoulder and dropped onto the blanket into a somersault.

Tom wheeled to a stop and watched the biggest boy pinning his two brothers to the blanket, flat on their backs.

Mrs. Emery stood to her feet, clasped Susanne's white glove between her hands, and pulled it close to her heart. "I don't know how we could put food on the table every day without your help. Thank you for your work at the pantry." Mrs. Emery bowed her head and tenderly smiled. "Thank you from my heart."

Susanne grasped the rear tires and said, "Thank you, and enjoy the rest of the celebration." She proudly wheeled around the blanket, stopped, and waited for Tom.

Tom removed his glasses and shoved his sweaty bangs to the top of his head. *If not us, then who?* popped back into his head as he glanced over at Susanne.

"My nose is running," sniveled the middle brother. "Let me go, Brendan."

Tom's attention fell back on Brendan as he released his brothers and said, "Yuck. Go get a hankie from Mom."

His brother scooted across the blanket, followed by the youngest brother. "Mom, I have boogies." He snuffed the dripping snot up into his nostril.

"Eeeuw," gagged the youngest brother.

Brendan turned away and gagged, "Eeeuw, yuck."

Tom slowly rolled by and smiled at the boy. Brendan ran from the blanket and tackled Tom's left leg. He sat on Tom's foot, wrapping his arms and legs around Tom's shin and tightly squeezing his grip. Tom froze still, sheepishly smiling, and his cheeks flushed red.

"Wow, Brendan really likes you," Mrs. Emery said.

"He must see something special in you." Susanne E. smiled.

Tom attempted to take a step with the young boy clinging tightly to his leg. He strained, lifting his foot from the ground and then plopped it down.

The boy laughed, snickered, and squeaked. "Do it again. Do it again."

Tom grinned and took several steps, lifting the boy into the air, stomped down, launched the boy upward, and flopped down.

The little boy tittered into a giggle and then chuckled into a belly laugh.

The stage lights flickered.

"Come over here, Brendan," called Mrs. Emery. "You have to let the boy go. The concert is about to begin."

Tom reached down and patted Brendan on the back. "Hey, little big man. I'll take a couple more steps, then I have to go."

The young boy smiled as he flew upward and flopped downward. "Higher. Higher," he hollered.

Tom stopped after several more strides. "Phew, I'm so tired," he said, wiping the sweat from his brow.

Brendan smiled, clinging tightly to Tom's leg.

Tom bent down, inches from Brendan's left ear. He cupped his hands around his mouth and whispered. Brendan clung tightly, not making a peep.

155

Tom then softly patted the young boy's back and tickled his belly in a circle. Brendan squirmed and wiggled, arching his head back and giggling towards the sky. The young boy never loosened his ironclad grip.

Mrs. Emery reached over, softly clasped her son's arms, and said, "OK. It's time to let go."

The boy squeezed tighter and began to whine as his mother wrenched his grip from Tom's leg. He arched back in an attempt to break out of his mother's hug. Brendan huffed and puffed, bloating his cheeks into a pout.

"Now, say thank you and goodbye," Mrs. Emery said.

"Enjoy the concert," Susanne said as she turned and made her way toward the oak tree.

Tom zigged his bike into the crowd and turned back with his index finger to his mouth. "Shush."

"Oh boy," Susanne said. "That little boy sure took a liking to you."

The oak tree and friends were twenty feet in front of Susanne when the sound of guitars tuning and drums beating ended.

Susanne turned to Tom and said, "We need to hurry."

"The Scent of Violets"
John W. Nassivera, Albert Bouchard, David Hirschberg

I can quote you some Samuel Clemens
His words echo down from the heavens
Forgiveness is like the sweet fragrance
Violets leave on the heel that crushed it

Jibber-jabbing about the day's events
Airbrushing the story of suspense
Sweeping hands and hearts a flutter
Puckered lips stammer and sputter
I leaned in close to Sally's ear
Whispered loud enough for all to hear

I can quote you some Samuel Clemens
His words echo down from the heavens
Forgiveness is like the sweet fragrance
Violets leave on the heel that crushed it

Stomping footsteps and a yelling frenzy
Sounding like jealousy and envy
The boys in a straight-line chime
Are you blind we've committed no crime
Hands speaking a tale of fury
We'll leave this to the judge and jury

I can quote you some Samuel Clemens
His words echo down from the heavens
Forgiveness is like the sweet fragrance
Violets leave on the heel that crushed it

Feeling her best, a smirk of triumph
Sally and the boys need an odd alliance
Anger only makes you smaller
Friendship is worth way more than the dollar
It's your chance to set the record straight

It's now time to deflate the hate

I can quote you some Samuel Clemens
His words echo down from the heavens
Forgiveness is like the sweet fragrance
Violets leave on the heel that crushed it

Chapter 20

A Cloud of Fury

Tom led Susanne forward to the oak tree. He thrust the kickstand down, and the bike teetered to a rest beside the Blue Lightning. "Ahem," Tom cleared his throat.

The boys' eyes were locked in on Cyndi as she held court, jibber-jabbing about the day's events.

Tom cleared his throat once again, "Ahem, ahem."

Cyndi's arms flailed through the air. Like a conductor of an orchestra, her hands swept and fluttered, airbrushing the excitement of her story.

159

"Hey, cool it with the yakking for a minute," Tom said. "I have someone I want you to meet."

Tom took a step to his right, revealing Susanne, and spoke over the low murmur of the crowded park, "You know Mike and Frank from the contest." He snickered and pointed. "Frank is the one slurping down my melting Creamsicle."

Susanne gently smiled and greeted Frank with an open gloved hand.

Tom swiftly reached out intercepting Susanne's hand. "I would advise you not to shake his icky, sticky orange hands with your white gloves."

"You took too long," slurped Frank as he gulped the last glop of creamy, frosty vanilla ice cream from the popsicle stick. "It started to melt." He leaned his head back and belched, "*Bwaaapurrrp*! I couldn't let a Creamsicle go to waste."

Mike slapped Frank on the shoulder. "That burp was a boomer."

The gunners chuckled as they gulped air and challenged Frank, *Bwwap, bwurrp, bwaurp.*

Cyndi nudged her way forward through the belch feast and said, "Your wheelies on the stage were the coolest."

Susanne E. leaned back into her chair and rolled the rear tires back and forth.

Cyndi leaned in close to Susanne's ear and whispered loud enough for all the friends to hear, "I've never seen anything like it."

The seven water gunners tromped forward in unison and, in cadence, said, "The coolest!"

"Yeah, you're the princess of wheelies in this village." Cyndi stood tall above the wheelchair. She waved an open hand like a wand to Tom, Mike, and Frank. "My three friends are so jealous."

"That was something else," Mike said, giving a thumb up. "Our bikes are made for wheelies, but I've never seen anyone pop a wheelie on four tires."

"Where did you learn how to hold a wheelie like that?" Frank asked. "Holding your front tires airborne was a showstopper." Frank rubbed his eyes, smearing orange gunk from his sticky grimy hands across his cheekbones. "I still can't believe my eyes."

"You must be talking about our race," Sally said from behind Susanne.

Tom wrenched his head to the right, kinking his neck. The muscles in the back of his neck pinched into a knot. "Ugh," he groaned, looking at Sally, and grumbled, "Yech..."

Sally stomped across a checkered pattern blanket, nearly squashing a catnapping Shih Tzu. The sudden pounding of her footsteps startled the pooch into a yelping frenzy as it chased after her heels. She trod off the blanket and trampled through a patch of beautiful purple and white violets woven through the green blades of grass. Sally marched to a halt and shoved Tom aside.

Sally stood erect beside Susanne with her arms folded across her chest and bellowed, "It was amazing how I left all three of you in the dust." She looked straight into Frank's eyes and said, "I thought your eyes were going to pop right out of your head when you almost ran that man over."

Cyndi's voice crackled, "Who... who..." she sputtered in anger. "Who invited her?"

"Yeah. Who invited her?" chimed in three of the platoon members as they filed into a straight line behind Cyndi.

Susanne rolled closer to Sally, sat upright, and proclaimed, "Tom and I did."

Mike pounced at Tom, practically leaping out of his skin. "What, are you crazy?" he hollered. "She almost got you arrested."

Frank charged in on Tom, cutting off any chance for escape. "Sally ran us off course, putting innocent people in danger."

Mike grabbed Tom's shoulder, and his voice trembled with outrage, "She cheated from the start of the race to the finish line!"

Frank turned to Sally, and his cheeks flamed red through the blotches of smudged orange Creamsicle. "Cheater!"

Sally calmly stepped to Tom, wearing a smile of satisfaction, and smirked, "I want to thank you for the invitation to join you and your so-called friends." She clapped her palms over her belly and chuckled. "I'm finding it funny they're all attacking you, when you all accuse me of being the wrongdoer."

The friends all became silent.

Sally turned her back to the group and said, "I didn't come here to make friends." She turned with a cruel smile and sneered at Tom. "We know how that worked out." She pointed at the three boys. "The three of you are the real cheaters."

"What?" Frank said, nearly jumping out of his shoes. "You're crazy!" He was inches from bumping noses with Sally and argued, "We never cheated in our lives."

"I'm crazy?" Sally asked, rubbing her finger across Frank's cheek.

Frank jumped back in a fuss, swung his hands in a cloud of fury, and barked, "Hands off."

Sally held her orange finger up in the air and waved it to and fro. "Not only are you a cheater, you're a liar." She stuck her orange finger inches from Tom's face. "What color do you see?"

Tom stood in silence.

Bobby ran, huffing and puffing from behind the wheelchair, into the center of the group. Sweat poured down his face, drenching his shirt. He arched his back and choked in three choppy breaths of air. "Orange," he grunted out.

"That's right, orange," Sally said. She slowly strolled to Susanne E. "I want to thank you and Tom for the chance to set the record straight." Sally ambled to the back of the wheelchair and clenched the handles. She slowly bent over and spoke into Susanne's ear, "Can you tell us if any of the TLCans were painted orange?"

Susanne tilted her head and squinted as she thought of Tom's question a few minutes ago. She gently touched her puckered pink lips and looked to Tom.

Tom's chin sunk into his chest, and he sighed in silence.

Frank burst forward, pushing Tom to the side. "It was a misunderstanding."

Mike said, "It was an honest mistake." He held his hands out to his side, saying, "We didn't know at the time."

Susanne calmly said, "What are you two talking about?"

Tom slowly raised his chin, looked into Susanne's eyes, and muttered under his breath, "I meant to tell you earlier." He meekly nodded. "We aren't sure, but we may have…" Tom gulped and began again. "We may have taken food from a TLCan and used it for our entry fees."

Susanne tilted her head to the other side and asked, "What do you mean?"

Bobby jumped in, shouting, "I heard the three of you with my own two ears! I was hiding behind the sky-blue can next to the stage." He pointed at Mike and Frank. "You two said you pulled the food out of the orange can. That was no accident."

Sally sprung to her toes, leaned out over Susanne's head, and hollered, "Tell the truth. You know what you did was wrong." She flopped back on her heels and smirked in triumph. "Cheaters."

Susanne E. rolled from under Sally to the center of the group. "Mistakes can be corrected." She looked up into Tom's sad puppy eyes. "That's why pencils have erasers."

Sally stomped onto the lawn between Susanne and Tom. Her shoes scuffed and scraped the grass, ripping and tearing the patch of violets from the ground. "How about we erase your win and you give first prize to the real winner, me?"

Bobby squeezed between Sally and Tom. He cupped his right hand over his left fist, squeezing, pulling, and bending his fingers. "Crrraack… Pop…Crack…" rattled from Bobby's knuckles. "Give up the cash," ordered Bobby as his chest bumped Tom in the face.

Tom's nose and mouth slid across the wet, slimy shirt and became buried in Bobby's sweaty pit stains. The sour stench of vinegar choked the air from his lungs as he inhaled. Tom wrenched his twisted face from the pit in disgust and gagged, "Pee-uw. What's that funk?"

Sally squawked, "The only thing that smells around here is you. Cheater!"

Tom held his hand up in the stop position. "Okay, the truth is we registered with three cans of creamed corn we took from a trash can on the corner of Elm and Oak Street."

"Cheater!" Bobby shouted.

Tom defended his confession. "We didn't know it was a TLCan until the middle of the contest."

Mike jumped in. "Frank and I were on our way to my house to grab three cans from Mom's pantry."

Frank lurched forward and confirmed it, saying, "We were running out of time when we came across this orange can full of food."

"It was the only way we could make it back in time to register," Mike said. "We didn't know. I swear."

Sally shrugged, clenched her fists, and kicked the ground, scuttling dirt and grass into the air. "Cheat, cheat, never beat," Sally chanted. "You lose, I win."

Blades of grass twirled like helicopters and floated to the ground. A single purple violet with a touch of white fluttered onto Susanne's lap.

"So, sweet," Susanne sniffed in the delightful aroma. "Here, Sally," Susanne said, offering the fragile violet.

Sally's face dropped out of anger. The group became silent.

"Mark Twain wrote, forgiveness is like the fragrance a violet leaves on the heel that stepped on it," Susanne said, extending her hand outward.

Tom looked at Susanne and said, "We read that in class."

Sally abruptly swung around, swooped down, and hovered over Susanne. "I thought you were going to be my friend," she growled through bared teeth.

Susanne smiled to the gnashing of Sally's teeth and softly said, "I would like that."

The grinding of teeth stopped immediately, and Tom witnessed the corners of Sally's mouth slightly turning up toward her cheeks for a second time.

Bobby burst out, "Hey, there's Mr. B. walking by a bench." He wildly jumped up and down, thrashing his arm in the direction of the fountain. Bobby jostled between Mike and Frank, waving and shouting to Sally.

"Follow me." Bobby jolted forward, bumping and elbowing a path through the troop.

A scowl fell over Sally's face. She glared at the three boys, curling her lips into an ugly twisted frown, and sneered. "Let's see what Mr. B. has to say about you three cheating." She ran after Bobby.

"Grant Me Friends"
John W. Nassivera & Bob Bates

Seated on a bench, legs tight and tense
Hand in a clench, leap with suspense
Bobbed to the left, then to the right
Look like a theft, fell out of sight

Over six feet tall, stood like a wall
Crank and haul, watched him crawl
Crouched like a lion, still as a stone
Pounced and flyin, land with a moan

Dangled from the string, sledgehammers swing
Dethrone like a king, it's time to sing
Hid behind a smile, drench head to toe
Waiting for trial, sadness and woe

Running from the heat, flee in retreat
Stopped in defeat, short of the street
Trapped and stranded, guns took aim
Captured red handed, innocent claim

Whatever you do, comes back to you
I'll give you a clue, it sticks like glue
Stand tall and honest, don't discourage
The first step is hardest, it takes great courage

Waiting to appeal, edge of his heels
Don't tease and steal, that's the deal
You're no different, than the others
Don't be a fool, we are all brothers

Wet cloud of mist, grant me a wish
Hands in a fist, don't resist
Crystal lens, clear as a gem
Grant me my friends, until the end

The Fountain by Kendall McKernon

Chapter 21

All Wet

168

The three boys stood shoulder-to-shoulder and stared down at their shoelaces like condemned prisoners, waiting for their execution.

Cyndi detached the squad. Each member of the troop held a water gun waist high with their fingers tightly bent around the trigger. Her orders rang out loud and clear, "Present arms."

The gunners held their water rifles tight to their shoulders.

The three boys raised their chins to the sky and closed their eyes.

"Shoulder arms," Cyndi barked out. The water gunners dropped their rifles back down to their sides. "Let's break camp and high step it over to the water hose at Bill and Harry's Gas Station." The troop marched off, two-by-two, under Cyndi's direction. "Let's shake a leg. I want everyone back in the park locked and loaded before the concert starts."

Susanne E. wheeled back and forth in front of the three boys, not saying a word.

Tom lowered his head and broke the silence, "I started the day wanting to make my dream come true." He sighed, slapped his right thigh, and stepped in front of Susanne. He grabbed the armrest and stopped the chair in its tracks. "But instead, I'm stuck in a nightmare."

"My mom told me that when things are dark and gloomy, the light switch is right in front of your face," Susanne said.

Mike scrunched his eyebrows and rubbed the top of his head. "I don't know about flipping on any light switch, but I sure would like to flip out on Bobby and bop him right in the belly."

Frank spat onto his shirt sleeve and wiped it across his cheeks, scrubbing the crusty orange paste from his face. "I wish I was bigger, so I could wallop Holler."

Susanne pushed upward to the front of the seat and said, "Anger only makes you smaller."

"Are you crazy?" Tom asked. "Sally didn't forgive us for making a mistake. Why should we forgive her and Bobby?"

"Sally and Bobby didn't take the three cans." Susanne flopped to the back of the seat. "The three of you did."

The boys were silent.

"Listen up. I've got an idea." Tom looked to Susanne, saying, "It's time we fessed up to what we did."

"What?!" Mike said. "Are you kidding me?"

Frank step to Susanne and said, "Susanne is right. We have to become bigger people and do the right thing."

Tom said, "We should have said something to Mr. B as soon as we found out."

"It was a mistake," Mike said. "We've been over this."

"The mistake is that I didn't say anything because I really, really want the Project J-38." Tom's hands closed into a tight ball, and he said, "But there was something that I wanted more." His shoulders tensed, and his jaw clenched. "We have to muster up the courage to tell the truth."

Mike pointed at the fountain. "Look at the head start they have."

Frank reached out and grabbed Mike by the shoulders. "We can do this. We're a team."

"Frank's right," Tom said, placing his hands on Frank and Mike's shoulders. "If we split up, we can quickly cover more ground." He clapped his hands together, cheering them on. "We have to get to Mr. B first." He then slapped both palms to his thighs, fired up. "We have to tell him before the concert."

"I'll stay here with the bikes," Susanne said. "That way if Mr. B gets by you guys, I can stop him before he gets to the stage."

"Great. Thanks for having our backs." Tom smiled. He raised his hand, pointing out to the fountain. "Now, let's go!"

Mike ran several strides in the direction of St. Mary's Church and jumped the curb onto Main Street. The street was clear. Most of the people in the village were already seated in the park, waiting for the concert. "I know someone who can help," Mike said.

Tom took flight, sprinting into the crowd. He bobbed and weaved a path past the stage. Frank jiggled and joggled through the crowd, circling west around the fountain.

Tom squirmed his way to the circular fountain in the center of the park. "Excuse me, coming through," he apologized. The pool of water stretched thirty feet across. An ornamental statue rose upward in the center, spraying a cloud of mist over the pool. He spotted Bobby halfway around, seated on a bench.

Bobby bent over, tying his sneaker laces, when, all of a sudden, he leaped from his seat. His eyes sparkled, and his red tongue fell out of his mouth. Then, he vanished.

"Shucks." Tom bobbed to the left, then to the right. "Where did he go?" He broke into a tizzy and flailed through the crowd. Out of the corner of his eye, he saw Frank jumping up and down. Tom waved his hands high in the air and mouthed the question, "Do you see Bobby?"

Frank pointed downward and waved Tom forward.

Tom rushed three strides forward and skid to a stop. A cold sweat ran down his cheeks. There stood Officer Thompson, the same policeman who had threatened to arrest him at the race earlier in the day.

The officer stood like a wall at six feet, two inches. Lucky for Tom, the policeman was busy, focusing on some mischief in front of him. Tom stood still and watched as the officer took a choppy step left, stutter stepped back to the right, and then shuffled back to the center of the sidewalk. Officer Thompson continued to sway and totter. His right arm reeled in a circle, as if he was fishing.

"That's it." Officer Thompson slowed his reeling. "Keep coming, take the bait."

Tom softly tiptoed to the policeman's left, remaining careful not to disturb the officer's land angling. He silently took two more steps and spotted Bobby crawling on his hands and knees toward them. Bobby's tongue flopped out of his mouth. White, foamy bubbles slobbered around his lips, and drool dribbled from his chin, splattering to the concrete. He crept forward, panting like a rabid dog.

"Just a few more feet." Officer Thompson dragged the bait slowly across the concrete, hopped it twice, jumped it two feet in the air, and skipped it once.

Bobby froze in an attack position. Not a muscle in his body twitched, quivered, or shivered. He was still as a stone, crouched like a lion that was ready to pounce on its prey.

"I got you now," whispered the policeman as he gently whirled and softly twirled a string. A brown leather wallet that was connected to the end of the clear fishing line scraped and brushed across the rough concrete.

Bobby's eyes glared down on the wallet with a twinkle of delight as it inched across the sidewalk at a snail's pace. He sprung forward, swooped down with open hands, and closed his eyes. Bobby laid still, crushing his victim beneath his heavy body. He slowly opened his eyes, only to find his hands strangling the officer's ankles as he smothered the policeman's black patent leather shoes under his chest.

Tom watched as the officer hovered over Bobby with a smirk.

"Looking for this?" Officer Thompson asked. The wallet dangled from the string, swirling just out of reach.

Bobby inched back off the policeman's shoes onto his knees and folded his hands in prayer. "It's not what it looks like, sir." Bobby's eyes joggled in his head, searching for an escape route. He began to fidget, twirling his thumbs, and pleaded, "You have to believe me, officer. I wasn't gonna steal the wallet." He shook his folded hands and glanced to the left. "I was going to bring it to the lost and found."

Officer Thompson looked to the left over the top of Bobby at the fountain. "Is this the boy?"

Tom recognized two boys that were half Bobby's age sitting on the knee-high wall with their legs crossed. Water dripped off their drenched sneakers onto the concrete sidewalk. The boys swashed their hands in the fountain. The cool blue water rippled against the side and splashed to the sidewalk.

"Yep, he's the one," said one of the boys as the other nodded in agreement.

Bobby hooked his thumbs in the bottom of his shirt and stretched the fabric below the zipper on his trousers. "I don't know these two kids." He sneaked a peek to the officer's right. To his surprise, the two boys' mothers stood side-by-side, swinging their five-pound pocketbooks like sledgehammers.

"Don't even think about trying to get past us." They snarled and scowled.

Bobby turned back to the young boys and hid behind a phony smile. "I was just playing earlier," he said. He held his right hand out to the two boys and murmured, "No hard feelings?"

One of the boys splashed a wave of water onto the sidewalk in front of Bobby. The other said, "If you think we can't see through your fake smile, you're all wet."

Bobby pivoted and bolted from Officer Thompson. He dropped his head and charged in retreat like a runaway train but didn't get to far.

"Safeties off. Prepare to engage," commanded Cyndi.

A barricade of fully loaded water guns stopped Bobby in his tracks.

Bobby held his hands up and folded them on top of his head in surrender. "There's no need for this," he sniveled. "Why can't we be friends?"

"Save your confession for Officer Thompson," Cyndi said. "Troops, march."

Bobby hobbled back to Officer Thompson, dragging his feet and scraping the edge of his heels across the gritty concrete.

Chris nudged her plastic gun barrel into the center of Bobby's back and commanded, "Pick your feet up and get moving."

Bobby shuffled forward with his head drooping and his wrist crossed behind his waist. "That's no way to treat a prisoner," he whimpered.

"Pipe down and keep moving," Chris said. "Any more lip from you and I'll squirt you right where you're standing."

Bobby took several quiet steps and stopped, trapped between the water gunners, two angry moms, and policeman Thompson. Bobby looked up into Officer Thompson's eyes and said, "I confess, sir." He dropped his head, sniffled, and whimpered. "I was going to keep the wallet."

Officer Thompson said in his gruffly voice, "That wallet trick works every time." The officer smiled and tucked the wallet and fishing line into his back pocket. "I think there are lessons to be learned. The first lesson is that honesty is the best policy."

Officer Thompson pointed to the two young boys sitting on the fountain wall. "Let's try this again. Do you recognize these two youngsters?"

Bobby turned and faced the two boys on the fountain wall and peeped, "Never saw them before."

The two younger boys splashed away, drenching Bobby from his head to his toes. Bobby stood soaked to his underwear. His hair clung flat to his head as he spat water out his mouth.

The young boys halted the assault.

"I guess you haven't learned lesson one yet." Officer Thompson looked Bobby straight in the eyes. "Let's make this the last time."

Bobby's sneakers squished and sloshed as he stepped to the boys. "I recognize them," he mumbled. His eyes continued to stare at the officer's shoes. "I'm sorry for being a bully."

The two young boys answered with a deluge, swamping Bobby. "I don't think you mean it," said one of the boys. Water splashed like a tsunami from the fountain, knocking Bobby to his knees.

Officer Thompson had jumped back three steps, keeping his shoes dry. "Lesson two is whatever you do always comes back to you."

"I mean it." Bobby gagged, then said. "I won't ever be a bully again."

Frank slapped Cyndi a high-five and said, "That's better than walloping Holler any day."

The water gunners surrounded Bobby, squeezing shoulder-to-shoulder, constricting any escape. Bobby looked up and seven faces looked down, fixedly into his eyes.

"I mean it. I'm honestly sorry," Bobby said.

Tony stepped from the line and stood directly in front of Bobby and asked, "Now that you know what it's like, what do you have to say for yourself?"

The circle of gunners opened, leaving Bobby face-to-face with Officer Thompson, the two younger boys, and their moms.

Bobby slowly lifted his drenched head and hand combed his wet hair up and over his forehead. "Kids won't look at me because I'm big." He fiddled and twiddled with the bottom of his shirt, twisting and twirling it into a tight knot. "I've heard them calling me names behind my back. Cyclops, Paul

Bunyan, Jolly Green Giant, and Big Foot are just a few." Bobby released the stranglehold on his shirt. "When I'm mean and tough, kids see me, and they show respect."

Officer Thompson placed his hand on Bobby's shoulder and looked down into his eyes. "Is that the way you want to be seen?"

"No." Bobby slouched forward, dropping six inches in size. He turned from the officer and looked into the eyes of the water gunners. His lips quivered, "It's better than being alone."

"When I'm hurt or angry and want something to change," Officer Thompson said. "Quite often I need to make a change in me." He stepped behind Bobby. "The first step is always the hardest." Officer Thompson firmly clasped both hands on Bobby's shoulders and looked up into the sky. "When I was your age my mom gave me some advice, 'Always treat others as you want to be treated.'"

Bobby's body shivered, his head hung low, and he watched water droplets fall from his wet clothes. Without looking up, he said, "Now I know how bad I made you two feel." His head slowly rose, without blinking once, and his eyes looked straight into the boy's eyes. "I'm sorry for picking on you so I could feel better about myself."

"It takes courage to admit you were wrong," Officer Thompson said. "That's a huge first step."

Bobby lifted his chin from his chest, and water dripped from his earlobes. "Thank you, sir."

Cyndi stepped to Bobby with an open right hand and said, "Welcome to our troop of friends."

"You really mean that?" Bobby toweled the water running down his forehead with a wet shirt sleeve. He slowly turned to the line of water gunners, wary of retaliation.

The squad jolted into the stiff stance of attention, broke rank, and charged forward.

Bobby's knees began to quiver. The gunners circled Bobby. His body trembled in response. To his surprise, the troop greeted him with pats on his wet back, thumbs up, and handshakes.

"Yeah. We see you," Cyndi said. She placed her hand on Bobby's shoulder.

"Hey, Frank," yelled Tom over the welcoming party. "There's Mr. B, walking with a bag of barbeque chicken on the other side of the fountain." Tom jumped in place and pointed. "Sally is right behind him. We have to get to him first. Run!"

"Checkmate"
John W. Nassivera & Alan Dunham

An old man racked the hairs of a beard,
That sour mouth girl you all fear,
Tangling his whiskers into a tuft,
Is about to call your bluff.

Sweat rolled over Tom's pastel pale cheeks,
Off his chin down to his feet,
Here comes the pain, exploding like a rocket,
Eyes bulging from their sockets.

To your left, left, left-right-left,
Everywhere we go,
People wanna know,
Who I am, Where I stand.
To your left, left, left-right-left,
Everywhere we go,
People wanna know,
Is this my checkmate?

Clasped hands-in-hands, bracing for the storm,
Frank arrived ahead of scorn,
Thunder raged like Jekyll and Hyde,
Tom clenched and gulped his pride.

Squishing and squashing from the end of the line,
Bobby stiff as a board with arms at his side,
Without any evidence, they're innocent,
Sally clinched her fist, no time for nonsense!

To your left, left, left-right-left,
Everywhere we go,
People wanna know,
Who I am, Where I stand.
To your left, left, left-right-left,

John W. Nassivera

Everywhere we go,
People wanna know,
Is this my checkmate?

Mr. B tapped his foot and crossed his chest,
Let's hear what the boy has to say, make it your best,
Someone explain what this is all about,
I'll tell the truth; Tom strongly spoke out.

To your left, left, left-right-left,
Everywhere we go,
People wanna know,
Who I am, Where I stand.
To your left, left, left-right-left,
Everywhere we go,
People wanna know,
Is this my checkmate?
Is this my checkmate?
Is this my checkmate?

Chapter 22

Checkmate

Tom stooped down and clenched his knees. "Do you see them?"

"No," Frank said. "They couldn't have gotten too far in this crowd."

The sound of a rasping and grating voice resonated from behind the boys. "That yellow-haired girl with the sour mouth is right over there."

Tom arched upwards, with his head swiveled over his shoulder, and asked, "I'm sorry, but did you say you saw Sally?"

A man stood hunched over and intensely peered down at the ongoing chess match. He ran his hand through the frizzy, straggly hairs of his long beard, twisting and tangling the bristly whiskers into a tuft.

"Have you gone mad?!" a rotund eighty-two-year-old man hollered. His bald head glared red as he scowled up from the seat at the chess table. "Hey, keep quiet. I'm trying to think."

Tom stepped to the back of the bearded man and whispered, "Excuse me, sir, but can you point out that girl?"

The tubby, bald man place his portly fingers around his double chin and grumbled, "Quiet!" He pushed his knight forward.

Tom tugged on the bearded man's tattered shirt and asked once again, "Could you please point the girl out, sir? We're running out of time."

He pointed to the right of Frank. "She's walking to the big oak."

Tom respectfully bowed twice and said, "Thank you for your help."

Frank hopped and shouted, "I see her. Let's go."

The boys ran off into the crowd. "We have to catch Mr. B before the concert starts," Tom said to Frank. "Let's go straight to the oak tree and cut Sally off before she gets to him first."

Susanne E. sat at her post, diligently keeping watch for any sight of Mr. B.

"Is she here?" Frank asked, falling to his knees.

"No," Susanne said.

Tom leaned against the wheelchair, gasping to catch his breath.

"Look over there," Susanne said, pointing at the stage.

Frank jumped to his feet and spotted Mr. B chowing down on drumsticks and wings like he hadn't eaten for days. Mr. B stopped briefly to dab some barbeque sauce running down his chin with a brown paper napkin.

"We've still got a chance." Frank panted with his mouth wide open.

182

A deep, gravelly voice interrupted the three kids' chatter. "Hey, my new friend." Buck walked around the gigantic oak's trunk, holding a half-dozen bags of barbeque chicken. "Congratulations on your big win."

Tom half smiled and said, "I couldn't have won without your help."

Frank tugged Tom's shirt and said, "We've got to go."

"Well, now that you can afford that new Project J-38," Buck said, stopping beside Tom, "I would like to talk to you about parking the Sting-Ray in my garage with the rest of my collection."

Tom looked at Susanne with his eyes wide open and whispered, "What do I say?"

Susanne shrugged, not making a peep.

Tom quickly turned to Frank; whose jaw fell open.

"Uhmm," Tom said, twitching. "I don't think you have enough room in your garage for one more bike."

Buck shifted the six bags into one hand and chuckled. His open hand lumbered downward and plopped onto Tom's shoulder. "I'll make room for a bike like that."

Frank tugged the bottom of Tom's shirt and mumbled under his breath, "I'm going." He released his grip and ran off.

The weight of Buck's hand became heavy on Tom's shoulder, and he slumped into a slouch. He timidly looked up at Buck and said, "I have something I want to tell you." Tom began to march in place, stopped, and then stepped to the right and back to the left.

Buck lifted his hand from Tom's shoulder. "What is it?"

Tom looked to Susanne, feeling faint, and then turned back to Buck.

Buck frowned and said, "It looks like you need some time to think about it." He looked over the top of Tom's head and scanned the crowd. "I'm looking forward to the possibility of adding that one-of-a-kind bike to my collection." Buck waggled side-to-side then bobbed up and down. "Have you seen my 1930's Colson Flyer? I lent it to my daughter-in-law for the contest."

Susanne politely spoke up, "Your family is right in front of the stage." She pointed to the mom and three children.

"Oh, I see them," Buck said. "I was hoping the Colson Flyer might win the fifty dollars." He slowly turned to the grandkids.

Tom dropped his head and said with a mousy squeak, "I'm sorry, sir."

Buck's voice rolled off his tongue in a low, deep rumble, "The best bike won!" He clutched Tom's shoulder. "I'm proud of you, son."

Tom gave way under the pressure. His cheeks blushed, and he felt as if his heart dropped. "I don't deserve it, sir." Tom took a deep breath, gathering up his courage. "You see, me and my friends…"

Buck's Coke-bottle glasses magnified the twinkle in his brown eyes tenfold. He winked down at Susanne. "Thank you, darling, for pointing out my family," he said with a velvety hushed tone before turning. "If you'll excuse me, I have to hurry." He walked into the crowd and yelled back, "You all enjoy the music. That long-haired customer of mine is going to sing that song he sung in the shop." Buck then held a thumb up and said, "I can't wait."

Buck's three grandchildren scrambled from the blanket into his welcoming arms. The two younger grandchildren clambered up each pant leg as Brendan grabbed the bags of barbeque chicken. The children scuffled and tussled onto the blanket and jockeyed for their own personal bag. Mrs. Maggie Emery pulled the bags from her sons and placed a finger before her puckered lips to hush them quiet.

"Let's say grace before we eat." She shushed the children quiet with a wave. The boys knelt on the blanket with their hands folded. Mrs. Maggie concluded grace with, "Amen."

The boys bowed their heads and said, "Amen." With a sudden swoop, they lunged forward with arms outstretched and nabbed their dinner.

"Whoa, that was close," Tom said. He turned to Susanne, saying, "I didn't know what to say."

Susanne said, "I don't know if it matters." She pointed at Frank, who was running back.

Tom choked, "Oh, no."

"What's This All About"
John W. Nassivera & Bob Bates

Seen once in a blue moon
Born holding a wooden spoon
Having an unquenchable thirst
But the truth should always come first

Looking to take a stand
Conflicting what's in my hands
Reaching for the sky
For something money can't buy

I know what it's like
Being different, not alike
If you see me for me
We'll all be set free

Falling from the heavens
Rolling lucky sevens
Landing flat on a seat
I'm standing without my feet

Offering open hands
With Tender Loving Cans
Living the golden rule
Smiling bright like a sparkling jewel

I know what it's like
Being different, not alike
If you see me for me
We'll all be set free

Standing bigger than a house
Not scared by a little mouse
Pushing up in everybody's face
Causing roadblocks for the human race

186

Chain Links

Don't call me Jolly Green Giant
I'll push back in defiance
I'm not wet behind my tears
I just want to stand beside my peers

I know what it's like
Being different, not alike
If you see me for me
We'll all be set free

Everything is in place
Curtsy with stylish grace
Wanting first at the show
Tired of living in someone's shadow

Two steps forward and cried out
Why would there be any doubt
It all makes, common sense
All anyone needs is confidence

I know what it's like
Being different, not alike
If you see me for me
We'll all be set free

If you see me for me
We'll all be set free
If you see me for me
We'll all be set free
If you see me for me
We'll all be set free
If you see me for me
We'll all be set free

Chapter 23

What's This All About?

The Sting Ray rested on its kickstand ten feet away next to the old oak. Tom fled for the bicycle and leaped onto the seat.

"What am I doing?" he asked himself. "I'm no coward." Tom slowly slid off the seat and trudged back, dragging his feet to Susanne's side. He stood red-faced and dug his fingers into the front pockets of his jeans.

"The truth may hurt at first." Susanne pulled Tom's left hand from his pocket. She cupped both her palms over the back of his hand as it rested on the arm of her chair.

"Well, here comes the pain," Tom said, nervously dancing in place.

Frank arrived first, out of breath. Droplets of sweat rolled over his rosy cheeks and trickled from his chin.

"Sorry," Frank gasped. "I was too late."

Tom patted him on the back, clasped his hand, and said, "Good try."

The three friends stood hand in hand as they braced for the storm to blow in.

Sally thundered through the crowd, stomping beside the yellow Roadster. Smiling from ear-to-ear, she said, "Reckoning day has arrived." She smirked and asked, "Where's your friend? Did he turn chicken and run home to his mommy?"

Tom crossed his arms over his chest and scrunched his eyes into a stare. "Don't worry about Mike. He'll be here."

Mr. B and Mr. Irish chatted as they ambled up to the group. Upon spotting Susanne, Mr. B smiled and politely said, "Hello, Miss Susanne E. Let me say that it's a true pleasure to have you as our Grand Marshall this year." He turned to Mr. Irish with a smile and said, "Ray, this is the young angel that has opened her arms to help those most in need in our community."

Mr. Irish bowed as he gently shook Susanne's gloved hand.

"What an honor it is to be in the presence of the brilliant, gifted genius that created the Tender Loving Can." Mr. Irish perked up, held his chin high, and poked his thumb against his puffed-up chest. "Being a professional engineer," Mr. Irish boasted, "I have the remarkable aptitude to deeply appreciate the blending of intelligence and artistry that it took to transform a trash can into a canister of love."

"Well said." Mr. B applauded while turning to Suanne with a smile. "A little long-winded, but so true." He winked at Susanne.

Sally tilted her head, frowning and grabbing the back of her neck. "Enough with the gooey stuff," she said. "Let's get on with it."

Mr. B and Mr. Irish slowly turned to Tom and Frank.

"I guess the reason we're here has nothing to do with our Grand Marshal, Susanne E.," Mr. B said with a frown.

"We should have known," Mr. Irish said, smirking. "Hey, where's that other kid?"

Tom dropped his shoulders into a slouch and answered, saying, "Mike will be here any minute." He looked straight at Mr. B and said, "You're right. This has nothing to do with Susanne."

"So, what's so important that it couldn't wait until after the concert?" Mr. B asked.

Sally grabbed Mr. B's arm and pinched so tight that his bicep tingled and blushed as red as a tomato with her fingerprints.

"Those boys are cheaters," Sally said.

"What are you talking about?" Mr. B. asked.

Sally pointed directly at the two boys and called out, "Those boys cheated. So, I win, and I want my first prize!"

"Wait one minute, Sally." Mr. Irish stepped between her and the boys. "You can't just accuse someone of cheating without any evidence."

Sally stomped her feet and hollered, "I'm telling you, they cheated!" She swung around, her right arm whizzed an inch past Tom's face, and she pointed to the stage. "I want you to go up on that stage right now and announce to the whole village that I'm the winner."

Tom and Frank stood still, white as ghosts and speechless.

"Well, Sally, Mr. Irish is right," Mr. B said. "Without any evidence, we can't accuse these boys of cheating."

The interrogation was interrupted by the pitter-patter of sneakers steadily beating like a drum. The steps grew louder, and a noisy chant trumpeted, "To your left, left, left-right-left."

"Now what?" Sally snarled. She squeezed the Roadster's handlebars and banged the front tire off the ground. "You have to be kidding me." Sally threw her hands into the air, and the bike crashed to the grass.

Frank pointed toward a fluffy clump of curly brown hair bopping above the seated crowd. "It's Cyndi and the water gunners," he said.

Cyndi led the platoon closer as she chanted in a singsong tone, "Everywhere we go-oh."

The gunners marched in two rows behind her, singing in unison, "People wanna know-oh."

"Who we are," belted out Cyndi. "Where we come from."

"So, we tell them," sung the platoon. "Mighty, mighty water gunners. From Sandy Hill."

The troop marched two-by-two up to the oak and filed into a single row, facing Mr. B. Bobby squished and squashed from the end of the line and stood at attention between commander Cyndi and Tom.

"Yuck!" Sally yelped, cringing at the sight of Bobby. "Ick! Gross!"

Mr. Irish tromped to a stop in front of Bobby. His chin sunk into his chest as he inspected the volume of water beneath Bobby's sneakers.

"What happened to you?" Mr. Irish asked.

"It's a long story," sniffled Bobby as the mud squished under his canvas sneakers.

"It's obvious." Sally stepped over her bike sprawled on the ground. "They took him prisoner and tortured him so he wouldn't tell."

Mr. Irish took one step back and pulled a square cotton handkerchief from his shirt pocket. He reached forward, padded Bobby's forehead, and swabbed the dribble from Bobby's chin.

"Is there something you want to tell us, son?" Mr. Irish asked.

Bobby stood stiff as a board with his arms at his sides, dumbfounded, and mumbled, "Huh? Like what?"

"Nothing?" Mr. Irish asked, resting his hands on his hips.

Bobby tilted his head to the side, and a drop of water dripped from his ear.

"Tell them, Bobby," Sally burst out. She ran to him, clenched his shirt collar in both hands, and demanded, "Tell them how those boys cheated."

Cyndi stepped to Sally and ordered, "Take your hands off our friend."

Sally released her grip, fell back a step, and cried out, "What have they done to you, Bobby?"

Bobby smiled with a faint glimmer in his eyes and said, "I've joined the troop." He waddled to Sally with open arms, saying, "Look at all my new friends. Why don't you join us?"

Sally clinched her fist and gave a loud, harsh, piercing cry, "They've brainwashed him!" She stepped to Tom and pushed her finger into his chest. "You're behind this," she said. Sally turned back to Bobby and pleaded, "Tell them the truth, Bobby. Tell them what you heard them saying."

Bobby stood open-mouthed and silent. He opened his hands at his sides and said, "But, these are my new friends."

"I'll tell the truth," Tom spoke out, stepping forward from the group.

Sally turned to Mr. B and said, "You can't believe him. He's a liar."

Mr. B. held up his hands and gently waved for Sally to calm down. "Now, let's hear what the boy has to say," he said. Mr. B crossed his arms over his chest and tapped his foot on the ground. "This better be good," Mr. B sternly said to Tom.

"Don't talk, Tom!" Mike shouted, pushing his way forward from behind the water gunners.

Mr. B slapped his hands to his head and grasped the few strands of hair left on his balding noggin. "What is going on here?" he asked, pulling the threadlike strands tight between his fingers.

Mike strutted up to Tom and Frank, followed by Attilio and several of the cooking staff.

"I have the answer for you, Mr. B," Mike said. He leaned into Tom and whispered, "I got this."

"Would someone please explain what this is all about before I miss the concert?" Mr. B asked.

Mike took a step nearer to Mr. B with a smile. "Let me introduce the inn owner." Mike turned with open hands. "He has the answer."

Attilio stood next to Bobby, wearing a stained white apron splatted with tomato sauce, splotches of olive oil, blots of red wine, and a daub of gelato.

Bobby's tongue rolled around the outside of his mouth as he reached over to rub a taste of ice cream from the owner's apron.

Attilio smacked Bobby's hand away and said, "Hey, rispetto." He frowned at Bobby and asked, "Che cosa e` una questione con te?"

"Huh," Bobby answered, wearing his normal, goofy look on his face and massaging his hand.

Mr. B politely requested from Attilio, "Could you say that in English, please?"

"Si," Attilio said, pointing to Bobby. "What's the matter with ragazzo? No respect."

Mr. Irish giggled from behind Mr. B and poked him in the back several times.

193

"Attilio," Mr. B said with a smile. "Can you tell us why you're here?"

"Si." Attilio waved the cooking staff forward. The one woman and two men stepped up, each carrying a huge one gallon can of creamed corn. Attilio pointed to Mike and explained, "Mio amico told me he was in guaio." He paused, holding his hand in the air for a moment, and continued, "Trouble and needed help. So, here I am."

The inn's owner pointed to the cans of creamed corn with a face of disgust. "We don't serve creamed corn in Italia." He pinched his nose closed and snorted, "Ha un odore di puke."

Two of the water gunners clasped their hands over their mouths, retching and heaving like they were vomiting. Bobby and the other gunners snickered, tee-heed, and giggled behind Attilio and his staff. Attilio then waved to his staff to set the cans down near Mr. B.

Mr. B turned to Mr. Irish, totally confused, and asked, "Is the entire community in on this?"

Mr. Irish shrugged and held his palms to the sky.

"Un minute," Attilio said, holding one finger in the air. His staff stepped forward holding three large jars. Attilio smiled and said, "I have brought three gallons of meatballs." He bowed and said, "Registrazione del concorso di tre amicos." Attilio clutched his chin and paused.

Bobby and the water gunners licked their chops and drooled at the sight of Attilio's famous meatballs.

Attilio scratched his head, turned to Mike, and asked, "How do you say in America?"

Chain Links

Mike shouted out, "Payment of the registration." He elbowed Tom and smiled with confidence. "I told you I got this."

Mr. B turned back and asked, "Can anyone tell me what is going on before this concert starts?"

Sally leaped for Tom's throat, stepping on her bike and snapping the chain in half. Mike and Frank jumped between them, blocking Sally from strangling Tom on the spot.

Sally hollered, "It's a cover up!" She bobbed and weaved in an attempt to get past Mike and Frank.

Tom pushed Mike and Frank to the side and stepped face-to-face with Sally.

"Tell the truth!" Sally shouted into Tom's face.

Tom stared into Sally's eyes and said loud and clear, "I need to get something off my chest."

"Is That a Smile I See"
John W. Nassivera & Bob Bates

Tom's hands slid down his jeans, over his hips
Upper front teeth bit down on his lower lip
Embraced his friends and slowly reached out
I've made some bad decisions there's no doubt
Not telling you after I won the contest
Keeping silent was dishonest I confess

We failed to pay, Tom fell to a knee humbled
Sally's jaw dropped, she stepped back and stumbled
If you can find it in your heart to trust
I would like to be your friend again Tom blush
The crowded park murmur, hushed, and listen
Sally search the ground for a decision

Is that a smile I see, sure looks it to me
A gentle heartened smile without limits
Is that a smile I see, sure looks it to me
The kind that raised another person's spirits

Lifted her head with a face flaming red
Slap Tom's hand away, wrestled past and fled
His ankle buckled, he fell out of sight
Bobby yelled hold tight with all your might
The pain of that day rolled up Tom's spine
That was my dream, Sally spoke her mind
Oh yeah… she did

Is that a smile I see, sure looks it to me
A gentle heartened smile without limits
Is that a smile I see, sure looks it to me
The kind that raised another person's spirits

Sally open up her hand with a gentle calm
The violet lay in the heart of her palm

Chain Links

It's not what you have that makes you rich
But what you do when you sew and stich
Sooner or later we're called to pay the price
For our friendship withstands cold and ice

Is that a smile I see, sure looks it to me
A gentle heartened smile without limits
Is that a smile I see, sure looks it to me
The kind that raised another person's spirits

Chapter 24

A Tightly Knit Circle

Tom's hands slid into his jean pockets and picked at some lent caught in the bottom of the lining. His upper front teeth bit down on his lower lip as his head dropped downward to Susanne E. She looked up with a gentle smile. It was a heartened smile, the kind of smile that raised another person's spirits.

He boldly said, "Sally is telling the truth."

Sally's jaw dropped. She took a step back and stumbled on the front tire of the fallen Roadster. She caught her balance and rushed to Mr. B, clinging to his arm and yanking him downward. Now face-to-face, she was looking Mr. B dead in the eyes. "I told you they were cheaters!"

Tom continued, without stumbling over a single word, "We failed to pay the registration. Those cans of creamed corn weren't ours."

He turned to Mike and Frank, firmly clasped them each by the shoulder, and looked straight into their eyes. "We found the creamed corn in an orange TLCan on Elm Street." He winked with confidence and whispered, "Team forever."

Tom turned back to Mr. B and confessed, "I was dishonest by keeping silent and not telling you after I won the contest." He stood between Mike and Frank, threw his arms over their shoulders, and embraced his friends. "We're sorry."

Tom slowly reached his hand out to Sally. "All I could think of all day was owning a new Project J-38 and showing off in front of the kids at school." His eyes dropped to the ground for a brief second. "I've made some bad decisions because of that." He moved his open hand closer to Sally and gently smiled. "I would like to be your friend again, if you can find it in your heart to forgive me."

Sally looked downward from Tom's face. Her eyes fixed on the toes of her shoes. She became quietly still.

The murmur of the crowded park seemed to go silent for a brief moment. It looked to Tom as if Sally was searching the ground for her decision.

"My bike!" Sally screamed.

She lifted her head, and her face was flaming red with anger. Sally slapped Tom's hand away, lowered her shoulder, and wrestled her way past. Just as Sally had arrived, she stormed away.

"Sally, wait!" Tom stumbled back a step, tripping on the tire of the fallen bicycle. His ankle buckled, and he plummeted.

"I got you!" yelled Bobby, lunging for Tom's outstretched hand. Bobby clasped Tom's fingers, yanking him to a stop. "Hold on!"

"Phew," gasped Tom. His rear end dangled an inch above the foot pedal. "Thanks."

"No problem," responded Bobby, wiping some sweat from his brow. "Sorry about making fun of you at school the other day."

The pain of that day started to rollup Tom's spine into his mind. He shrugged it off and said, "I accept."

They both took notice of the broken chain dangling off the gear teeth and dropped to their knees for a closer look. Bobby reached out and held the two ends in his open palms.

"How did this happen?" Bobby asked. "No wonder Sally ran off so upset."

Tom quickly looked out into the crowd for Sally. She was nowhere in sight.

Bobby pulled and yanked the ends in an attempt to push the broken link back together, but the greasy chain slid between his fingers and fell to the ground. "We have to fix this for Sally," he said with a blank look on his face. "If only we had some tools."

Tom pivoted to the stage in search of Sally and spotted Buck bouncing Brendan in his arms. "I got it," he hollered.

Bobby grabbed Tom's arm. His slimy, grease-covered hand slid down Tom's forearm, leaving a murky black streak. "Got what?"

Tom reached into his back jeans pocket, pulled the chain breaker out, and held it in front of Bobby's face.

Bobby squinted. "What's that?"

"The answer to our problem," Tom said with a smile. "It's a chain breaker."

"What good is that?" Bobby shook the ends of the broken chain in each hand. "The chain is already broken."

Tom shook his head back-and-forth. "Just sit there and watch."

He snatched one end of the chain from Bobby and cranked the knob on the breaker, releasing the link. He looked to Bobby and said, "Okay, this is where I need your help."

"You got it," Bobby said as he lurched forward. "What do you want me to do?"

"Squeeze the two ends of the chain together and hold them still until I connect the link."

Bobby grabbed the two ends, yanked, and pulled them until the holes lined up perfectly.

"Okay," Tom said. "Don't move."

Tom aligned the breaker over the end of the chain. He reached to turn the knob, and the ends of the greasy chain slid through Bobby's fingers and fell to the ground.

Bobby moaned, "Sorry."

Tom patted Bobby on the back and said, "No problem. We'll just try again."

Bobby dropped his head and knelt over the broken bike in defeat.

Tom put his hand on Bobby's shoulder, leaving a grease smudge. "But first, wipe the grease from your hands."

Bobby smiled as he rubbed his thighs, smearing his pants with grease. He seized the chain and clutched the ends. Bobby snatched and jerked the ends together. His shoulders and biceps began to quiver as he strained to hold the chain perfectly still.

Tom began to twist and turn the knob.

Sweat dripped from Bobby's forehead and splattered on the breaker, causing Tom's fingers to slip off the knob.

"Hold tight with all your might." Tom groaned as he ratcheted down on the knob.

The chain breaker clicked and clanked, sealing the chain together.

Bobby fell back on his butt, sweat dripping off his forehead, and shook a cramp from his hand. Tom flopped down next to Bobby and moaned with relief.

"Now that's teamwork," Tom said while giving Bobby a high five.

Tom jumped to his feet, lifted the bike from the ground to its tires, and pushed into the crowd. He looked back at Bobby rejoining the group. To Tom's surprise, he spotted Sally over Mike's left shoulder, ten feet away and sitting with her back against the oak tree. Tom wheeled the Roadster up to Sally and bumped her foot with the front tire.

Sally kicked the bike away without taking a single glance.

Tom said, "Will you forgive me? I really would like to be friends."

Sally sadly turned her head, ignoring Tom.

"I didn't have any money for the rides at the bazar," Tom said. "I felt like a loser."

Sally sat in silence.

"You wouldn't understand," Tom said. "Your dad has all the money in the world."

Sally turned her head and came face-to-pedal with the repaired chain. She rolled from the tree, quickly crawled to the chain, and examined the fix.

Tom shouted down at Sally, "I couldn't have fixed it without Bobby's help!"

The corner of Sally's mouth slightly rose as she continued to inspect the chain. She tugged the link, and the chain held together, tightly wrapped to the gear teeth.

"Is that a smile I see?" Tom asked, smiling down.

Sally jumped to her feet and pressed her index finger into Tom's chest.

"You still cheated," she snarled. "I wanted to win just like my dad did."

Tom wrenched the kickstand down and parked the bike. His forehead wrinkled upward above the rim of his glasses. He opened his arms to his sides and said, "Sally, I'm sorry."

Sally clenched her hands around the Roadster's handlebar and stared at the front tire. "That was my dream," she said. "You ruined it."

Tom quietly looked at Sally, biting his tongue in silence.

Sally slowly peered out to the bandstand and said, "For the last six months, I dreamed about winning the competition. Standing on the stage and accepting first prize in front of the entire village. The crowds of neighbors cheering for me." Sally paused, completely motionless, like a manikin in the store front of W.T. Grants department store.

 Tom took in a large breath and remained silent.

Sally continued to glare at the bandstand. "The villagers' cheers would silence, and Mr. B would ask 'What are you going to do with the fifty dollars?'"

Bobby ran up behind Tom and placed his hand lightly on the back of Tom's shoulder. He whispered into Tom's ear, "Is Sally alright?"

Tom held his finger to his lips and shushed Bobby quiet.

Sally continued to stare ahead, not taking notice of Bobby's arrival. "The village would be completely silent. You would hear the chirping of a blue bird in the tree above the stage."

The two boys stood motionless, completely silent. Mike, Frank, Cyndi, and the gunners quietly walked up behind Bobby and stood without a peep, intently listening to Sally.

"That's when I would announce to the whole village that I was giving the money to Doreen's Food Pantry." Sally cupped her left hand to her ear. "The village would erupt into cheers and applause so loud that all of the Town of Kingsbury would know that I gave the winnings to charity." Sally sniffled, and her body shivered. "You don't know how hard it is being the daughter of the richest man in town. People think everything is given to you." She turned with a tear rolling down her cheek and said, "I can do just about anything, and it's not because my dad has money."

Susanne rolled next to Sally and gently wiped the tear from her cheek with her white glove.

Sally stood motionless. She reached her right hand out to Susanne and gently unfolded her fingers. The violet lay softly on her palm.

To Sally's surprise, the crew of friends rushed forward and enclosed her in a tightly knit circle. Everyone beamed at Sally with gleaming smiles.

Mike and Frank reached out with open hands. The two boys lifted Sally up onto their shoulders and bounced her high above the circle. The seven gunners sprayed a salute to the sky, emptying the water rifles in honor of another new friend.

Tom yelled up to Sally, "It's not what you have that makes you rich, but what you do that lifts you up."

The kids circled, jumping up and down and chanting, "Sally! Sally!"

The two boys took a knee, lowering Sally to the ground.

A voice from outside the circle chimed, "You have always been my champion."

The circle became completely quiet, and all eyes searched for the voice.

A tall man in a blue suit and a red tie gently made his way into the center of the circle. Sally's dad lifted her in his arms above his head and said, "You will always be the light of my life.

Hudson Falls…a Great Place To Call Home by Kendall McKernon

Chapter 25

Show the Love

The bandstand lights flicked on, and the crowd cheered for the start of the show. Buck's long-haired customer stood at the front of the stage in a rainbow tie-dyed T-shirt. He bent forward, nearly chewing on the metal screen cover of the mic. "Urmm… test, test, one, two, three."

Frank jumped with excitement, pointed to the stage, and hollered out, "Hey! He's wearing a T-shirt exactly like mine!"

Cyndi and the gunners blitzed Frank, covered his mouth with their hands, and whispered, "Shush."

The musician swung a leather strap over his shoulder and hung an electric folk guitar over the large silver buckle of his belt. His thumb swept up and down across the strings, strumming an E chord and then bar chords B and F sharp minor. Two guitarists and a bass player paraded onto the stage. A loud, harsh screech reverberated out of the speakers as they plugged into the system. The drummer jogged onto the stage, twirling the end of his moustache, and waved the sticks over his head at the crowd. A brief applause welcomed the band as he flopped to a stool behind the drum set.

The warm-up session came to a sudden stop, and the entire park became silent in anticipation.

The musician's voice belted out from the speakers, "Welcome to this year's Sandy Hill Day Celebration. I'm Jon, and we are the Music Hall Band." The villagers clapped. "We would like to open tonight's show with a song we recently learned." Jon pivoted to the members of the band, released the neck of his guitar, and threw them a thumbs-up of confidence. He swiveled on his heels back to the mic and said, "Most importantly, I think this song promotes a spirit of acceptance, respect, and cooperation as a community, so our faith and hopes for the future grow as one." The crowd put their hands together once again and applauded. The whistling and clapping rumbled to a silence.

"It's a Beatles song," Jon joyfully shouted into the mic.

A scream suddenly erupted within the audience, "*AwwwAAAAAAAAA!*"

All eyes dropped from the stage and became glued on the mom of three wildly jumping up and down in front of the bandstand. She waved a fistful of dollars above her head as she leaped toward the sky with joy. Her two youngest children scrambled across the blanket, clambered against her shins, and wrapped their legs into a stranglehold around her ankles. Maggie Emery sprung the boys upward off the ground and hopped in a circle. Her face lit up with glee as she screamed uncontrollable whoops of joy.

Buck jumped up next to his frantically screeching and shrieking daughter-in-law and lifted his grandson into his arms.

"It's the prize money!" Maggie cried out.

She tightly hugged Buck and Brendan and buried her head between them. She released her grip and tearfully shuffled through the dollars.

"Now we have money for food and clothes."

Buck turned toward the huge oak tree, stood tall with his chin up, chest out and shoulders back, and saluted Tom.

Tom's heart pounded like a bass drum in his chest. He thought, *This was what mattered. Not a new bike and showing it off to be cool at school.*

Tom looked back to Buck, and a smile stretched across Brendan's face as he threw Tom a salute.

Tom laughed to himself, jerked his shoulders back, thrusted his chin upward, and threw his little sidekick a salute back. "You're the man," Tom shouted, throwing a thumb up into the air.

"One, two, three…," blared out to the crowd from the wall of speakers and the concert began.

Tom felt a tug on the back of his shirt. It was Mr. B, standing with an extended open hand. "I see you discovered the power of giving."

Tom shook the principal's hand and said, "If not us, then who?"

"What's that?" Mr. B asked.

Tom puffed his chest out and threw his shoulders back. "No matter how rich or how poor we think we are, we have the power to choose to make a difference."

Susanne said, "You already had the best bike." She shifted the 5-speed into first gear.

"You're right there," Tom said, "I think I'll keep her." He lifted his head and smiled ear-to-ear. "Nobody can beat the Sting Ray."

Sally giggled from off to the side and said, "I don't know about that." She walked up to Tom. "You tell me when and where." Sally held out an open hand and smiled. "I'll be there."

"Oh. It's on." Tom smiled. He grasped her hand. "Friends."

"By the way." Mr. B grabbed Mike and Frank by the shirt sleeves and pulled them next to Tom. "I'll see all three of you in my office on Monday for lunch detention." He released his grip. "We need to resolve this issue about the three cans of creamed corn."

The boys looked at each other. Mike sighed and whispered to Frank, "Prison."

"I know just how the three of you can make this right." Mr. B pointed to the sky-blue Tender Loving Can. "Doreen's Soup Kitchen & Food Pantry needs help stacking and stocking all the cans of food that were donated."

Mike slumped behind Frank and quietly groaned, "Hard labor."

"Mike, make sure you bring your older brothers," Mr. B said. "They owe me some work."

Tom smiled and slapped the two boys a high five. "No problem, Mr. B," he said. "We'll be there right on time, and you can count on us doing the job right." Tom smiled at Mike and Frank, saying, "Teamwork."

"See you Monday." Mr. B walked over to Mr. Smite and tapped him on the shoulder. "Let's go join Mayor Muff." The two made their way through the crowd to the front of the stage.

Susanne smiled. It was a subtle, gentle smile, but irresistible, the kind of smile that spread from one person to another. Susanne yelled out, "Now that's, 'SHOWING the LOVE!'"

Jon and the Music Hall Band played on, and the chain of friends joined the entire village in singing the chorus. In the words of the Beatles, those famous musicians who had risen to worldwide fame:

"I get by with a little help from my friends."

End Of A Perfect Day by Kendall McKernon

John W. Nassivera

"Show the Love"
John W. Nassivera & Alan Dunham

Coming together through song
The bandstand lights flicked on
The musician belted out
As he threw two thumbs-up

The crowd cheered out and beyond
In a spirit community strong
The band lined across the stage
Faith and hope turns the page

Show the Love
With a gentle smile
The kind that shines for miles
Oh. It's on
Show the Love
Shine for every mile
Pave the way for more smiles

A time to join hands and play
Light up one another's day
Help someone in need
Take a moment to be free

No matter how rich or poor
Choose the power to cure
It doesn't matter when or where
Just choose to be there

Show the Love
With a gentle smile
The kind that shines for miles
Oh. It's on
Show the Love
Shine for every mile

Chain Links

Pave the way for more smiles

Don't hold onto a bad memory
Use it for discovery
Find the power of giving
Lend a hand and start living

You can count on us
It's a matter of trust
From all different ends
We all become friends
When we…

Show the Love
With a gentle smile
The kind that shines for miles
Oh. It's on
Show the Love
Shine for every mile
Pave the way for more smiles
Show the Love
Shine for every mile
Pave the way for more smiles

THE END

Creating Community One Story at a Time, by complementing the good our neighbors are doing so that the good continues.

John W. Nassivera

My approach to book writing is rooted in the community building shared on the front porches many of us grew up on. Our neighbors' stories of innovated and creative actions to better their communities can inspire us all. When we engage in complementing their work and design our own original approach to building community, we are writing the next chapter in our own story.

www.frontporchstorytelling.com

Meet the neighbors.

Albert Bouchard

When I was a teen, I had a band with my brother, Joe. In college, I formed a band with Don Roeser that became Blue Öyster Cult. I left BOC in 1982 and worked as session musician and musical director for oldies acts. I went back to college and got my BA in music and MA in English Literacy. In 2008, I formed a band with Joe and Alice Cooper bass player Dennis Dunaway, called Blue Coupe. In 2016, President Barack Obama honored me at the White House as an outstanding educator. Since 2006, I've recorded Fabienne Shine, Spirits Burning and others and have a vlog called Most Cowbell!!!

http://www.albertbouchard.net/

Robert Bates

Robert Bates was born March 4th, 1954 in New York City. He attended The Juilliard School, where he received a bachelor's and master's degree in music. He also attended Hofstra University, where he received his teacher's certificate. Mr. Bates has been singing, composing and conducting music for over 40 years. His compositions in chamber music have been published by Paul Price Publications, and his piece "Blue Offering" has been played in South America and Europe. In 1994, Mr. Bates joined Opry star Charlie Louvin and performed with Charlie on the Grand Ole Opry and around the country for several years. Mr. Bates is currently working with his songwriting partner JoAnn Sifo and the Dyer Switch Band. They are performing their original songs around the country and are receiving a great deal of radio airplay, including the song "I Just Can't Stay," which reached #20 on the Sirius radio charts. He also writes songs with his partner Debra Hall, and he currently resides with her in Hudson Falls, NY.

www.dyerswitch.com

Alan Dunham

Alan Dunham is the owner of Lylac Studios, a recording studio located in South Glens Falls, NY. Aside from engineering recordings for artists, Alan is a musician himself and has been writing songs since he was 13 years old. Currently, he performs in a duo with Elizabeth Winge, with whom he has released several recordings. As a member of the Strand Theater House Band at the newly renovated Strand Theater in Hudson Falls, NY, he often takes part in tribute shows. Mr. Dunham is a published songwriter and enjoys working with the public. More info about him and his recording studios can be found on https://www.hudsonwaves.com/.

David Hirschberg

David Hirschberg was born in New York City in 1955. Music was always a part of his life thanks to his mother, who was an alto in her leisure time. He has played clarinet, alto & tenor sax, bassoon, guitar, and bass. Mr. Hirschberg is drawn to the bass because it brings together and compliments both rhythm and melody.

Kendall McKernon

I spent many years as a professional interior designer but am now devoting myself to the art of photography. Based in the foothillls of the Adirondack Mountains in upstate New York, many of my photos highlight the beauty and rich history of my community and the region. I also have a deep love of New England and the coastal areas just hours from my home, so I am broadening my portfolio with photos of those areas, as well.
In October 2016, I opened The McKernon Gallery at 216 Main Street, Hudson Falls, NY. The Gallery is filled with wall, functional, and wearable art that features my photographs. The inventory is constantly changing, so each trip in is an adventure for customers.

http://kendallmckernon.com/

John W. Nassivera

A Special Thanks for their contributions.

Jonathan Newell keyboards
> Ready Set Go
> Stopped Red Handed
> Is That a Smile I See

Stu Kirby keyboards
> Show the Love

Sal Viola percussion
> As We Get Boulder
> Click! Snap! Pop!
> Don't Stop
> Rules Are Rules
> Stick to the Plan
> It's Show Time
> Ready Set Go
> Stopped Red Handed
> Many Friends
> What's This All About
> Is That a Smile I See

Elizabeth Winge vocals
> It's Show Time
> Feeling So Cool
> The Scent of Violets
> Checkmate
> Head in A Haze
> What's This All About
> Show the Love

Dakota Bates vocals
> Ready Set Go

JoAnn Sifo vocals
> What's This All About

Gisella Montanez-Case vocals
> It's Show Time

220

Made in the USA
Columbia, SC
21 October 2024